WITH THE FLICK OF A KNIFE . . .

For a moment, Tharp stared down at his knife and at the blood that was on it. He peered at Joe Moss, but there was no blood on Joe's belly. Finally Tharp seemed to notice the small, red, sausage-like piece of meat that lay close to his fallen knife. Then he looked, mutely, at his own right hand—or what was left of it. The thumb that had been wrapped tight around the haft of the long Arkansas knife was gone. It simply was no longer there.

Tharp looked up at Joe again and seemed finally to realize what just happened. He tilted his head back and let out a long, quavering scream.

Then again he charged forward, perhaps intending to batter Joe down with sheer hate. Perhaps with no coherent thought, only an unformed desire to club and to kill . . .

MAN OF HONOR

A Joe Moss Novel

GARY FRANKLIN

BERKLEY BOOKS, NEW YORK

THE BERKLEY PUBLISHING GROUP
Published by the Penguin Group
Penguin Group (USA) Inc.
375 Hudson Street, New York, New York 10014, USA
Penguin Group (Canada), 90 Eglinton Avenue East, Suite 700, Toronto, Ontario M4P 2Y3, Canada
(a division of Pearson Penguin Canada Inc.)
Penguin Books Ltd., 80 Strand, London WC2R 0RL, England
Penguin Group Ireland, 25 St. Stephen's Green, Dublin 2, Ireland (a division of Penguin Books Ltd.)
Penguin Group (Australia), 250 Camberwell Road, Camberwell, Victoria 3124, Australia
(a division of Pearson Australia Group Pty. Ltd.)
Penguin Books India Pvt. Ltd., 11 Community Centre, Panchsheel Park, New Delhi—110 017, India
Penguin Group (NZ), Cnr. Airborne and Rosedale Roads, Albany, Auckland 1310, New Zealand
(a division of Pearson New Zealand Ltd.)
Penguin Books (South Africa) (Pty.) Ltd., 24 Sturdee Avenue, Rosebank, Johannesburg 2196,
South Africa

Penguin Books Ltd., Registered Offices: 80 Strand, London WC2R 0RL, England

This is a work of fiction. Names, characters, places, and incidents either are the product of the author's imagination or are used fictitiously, and any resemblance to actual persons, living or dead, business establishments, events, or locales is entirely coincidental.

MAN OF HONOR

A Berkley Book / published by arrangement with the author

PRINTING HISTORY
Berkley edition / July 2006

Copyright © 2006 by Frank Roderus.

ISBN: 0-425-21077-4

BERKLEY®
Berkley Books are published by The Berkley Publishing Group,
a division of Penguin Group (USA) Inc.,
375 Hudson Street, New York, New York 10014.
BERKLEY is a registered trademark of Penguin Group (USA) Inc.
The "B" design is a trademark belonging to Penguin Group (USA) Inc.

PRINTED IN THE UNITED STATES OF AMERICA

10 9 8 7 6 5 4 3 2 1

✛ 1 ✛

"I'VE A MIND to cut your liver out an' feed it to my dog, damn you." The voice came from the other side of one of the big Conestoga wagons. Joe Moss reined his paint to a halt and frowned.

"I was only—"

"You shut your mouth if you want to keep living," the first voice said again, deep and rough and definitely, as if this was no idle threat.

Moss wheeled the paint around the back of the wagon and found two men there, both dressed in rough clothing, one of them a man with graying hair who nonetheless was very large and powerful-looking. He had bulging forearms and held a butcher knife in his fist. He was holding the point of the knife tight to the throat of a much younger and smaller man, who had come onto his tiptoes to keep the blade from piercing his flesh. The man with the knife had his other fist locked around a handful of the smaller fellow's shirtfront so he could not move away.

"I only—"

"One more sound, you sonuvabitch, and you'll die in the dirt right here an' now," the older man rasped.

Moss touched the paint's ribs lightly with the heel of his moccasin and positioned it beside the two men before he tightened his rein again. He pulled the horse's neck around so he stood sideways to the pair. As if by coincidence, this placed the muzzle of his plains rifle on a line with the head of the man holding the knife.

"Afternoon, gents."

"Go away, mister. You ain't wanted here," the big man said.

Moss grunted. "I can see how I might not be, but I want to warn you about something. The sight of blood, it kinda upsets me. Do I see any of it, I'm just real likely to squeeze down on the trigger of this here old rifle gun. By accident, you understand. Damn shame too, because then there'd be two fellas lying dead in the dirt here. D'you take my meaning, mister?"

The rifle lay across Moss's lap and was about on the same level as the throat of the fellow with the knife. The weapon was .54 caliber and from that distance and angle probably looked like a cannon with a bore big enough to crawl into.

"I told you, mister—"

"So you did," Moss said, his voice hard now. "And I'm telling *you*. Put that knife away or I'll decorate the canvas of this here wagon with whatever few brains you got."

"You can't talk to me like that."

"I just did," Moss said.

"You wouldn't if you didn't have that gun in your hands."

"Put the knife away," Joe said softly. "I don't much like having to repeat myself."

"Who the hell do you think you are anyway?"

"Apart from the being the person who just may kill you,

my name is Joseph Moss—that'd be *Mister* Moss to the likes of you—and I'm the master of this here wagon train. And if you expect to get t' the Californias, you'd best hope I don't decide t' either shoot you or throw you the hell outa this train. Now for the last time, mister, put that knife down. An' let go of him."

Joe gestured with the muzzle of the rifle, and reluctantly the big man relinquished his hold on the other and lowered the knife.

"You're just lucky you had that gun in your hands."

The smaller man bolted, turning tail and scampering away without taking time to thank his benefactor. Moss stepped down off his Mexican saddle and dropped his reins in the dirt. The horse lowered its muzzle and acted like it was tied in place there.

On that bright and sunny Missouri afternoon, Joe Moss was thirty-seven years old, tall and lean, with piercing blue eyes and hair so black and glossy it looked like it had been oiled. His complexion was ruddy, burned red by years of constant exposure to sun and wind. He wore a fringed doeskin hunting shirt that fell almost to his knees, woolen trousers, and soft, beaded moccasins. He had a scarlet sash into which he'd stuffed a sheathed bowie knife, a brace of horse pistols, and a tomahawk. Leather thongs crisscrossed his chest supporting a bullet pouch on one side and a possibles bag on the other. A ragged scar traced the left side of his jaw.

Joe stepped away from his mount and propped the barrel of his rifle against the side of the wagon. He turned to the big fellow, who was still holding the butcher knife, and said, "Well, now, would you looka here. Seems I don't have any gun to protect me now. Whatever d'you think of that?"

The big man gave Moss a wary look. Then his anger returned and his resolve hardened. "You sonuvabitch!" He raised the butcher knife again and took a step toward Moss.

The bowie flashed in Joe's hand, the big knife held balanced almost loosely on his palm, not clutched tight in his fist, the cutting edge upright and point elevated. Moss dropped into a slight crouch, knees bent and with his weight balanced on his toes, and moved forward toward his adversary.

The man began to look nervous. "Look . . . mister . . . I never meant . . . I never said. . . ."

"Fight or back water, but I'm telling you straight out you done went too far calling me that. Now you choose what you want to do and we'll have at it."

"I . . . I'm sorry. I take it back. I never meant nothing by it. I swear that I never."

"Down."

"What?"

"You. Get down. On your knees."

The man glanced nervously to one side and then the other. The fellow he'd just been bullying had come back, and a dozen or more other members of the train with him. "I can't . . . I can't . . . Jesus God, mister, everybody's watching. I can't get on my damn knees. You can't 'spect me to do something like that."

"Do it, mister, or I'll give you a look at your own guts laying on the grass where you stand. But that's up to you, isn't it. Make up your mind an' do it right now." Joe inched forward, his bowie gleaming wickedly in the sunlight.

"Jesus, mister, I . . ."

Joe came half a step closer and the big man went pale. With a gasp, he dropped the butcher knife and fell to his knees. "I'm sorry. I swear to God I never meant anything by what I said. I'm sorry."

Joe looked around to make sure the other men were getting an eyeful. He grunted. "Fine. Get up an' get out of my sight. No, leave the knife right there. And mister. You aren't traveling with this train no more. I don't need t' have your kind around, so pull your rig outa line."

"But . . ."

The big man stood and Joe moved in on him again, the bowie still held ready. "No argument. Just git."

"Yes."

"Yes what?"

"Yes, sir. Mr. Moss. Can I . . . can I have my knife back?"

"If you're man enough to pick it up an' use it. Otherwise, turn tail and skedaddle."

The fellow's breathing was fast and shallow, and cold sweat beaded his forehead. He turned and scurried away, leaving the knife on the ground where it lay.

✤ 2 ✤

JOE RODE SLOWLY through the massed wagons. They were as fit and ready as he could make them and as lightly loaded as he could cajole their owners into packing them. Inevitably, there were too many items being carried, precious keepsakes and furnishings. Nearly all of those would be discarded along the way. Joe knew that. The owners of these rigs did not. Yet.

Even so, he was satisfied, or as much so as was possible on this clear, cool morning. Sixty-three wagons, each filled with hopes and dreams as much as with foodstuffs and clothing and the tools that would be needed to start new lives when they reached their far-off destinations. That would take place some months in the future depending on grass and weather and the many choices that would have to be made along the way. The responsibility for those choices was Joe's and his alone.

The company was starting as early in the season as Joe felt there should be graze available along the way. But then

a bull train is slow. Oxen are steady pullers and durable if
their feet are properly cared for. Horses are faster, but in
the long run more tender. And the horses certainly are of
more interest to Indian thieves. An Indian will steal a horse
for the sheer pleasure of it, but will want an ox only if he is
hungry.

Joe approached the wagon belonging to the president of
the emigrant company and reined the paint to a halt. Mrs.
Kramer sat perched on the wagon seat with a heavy shawl
wrapped around her shoulders. She was shivering a little,
probably chilled but perhaps from plain nervousness. Sam
Kramer stood beside the rig and his son was with their lead
ox, holding a goad and looking excited.

"Ma'am." Joe removed his hat and nodded. "Soon as
the sun is properly up, ma'am, it'll start to warm." He replaced the hat and turned his attention to her husband. "Are
your people ready, Sam?"

"As ready as we can make them, I think."

"Did Hallett get rid of his wife's chiffonier?"

Kramer grinned and shook his head. "You know better."

Joe shrugged. Mrs. Hallett treasured that damn chiffonier above all. Joe suspected she would rather abandon
their food than her heavy, ornate, utterly worthless bureau.
He had told Benjamin a dozen times to get rid of the thing,
but the man would not—or could not—do so against his
wife's will. So be it, Joe figured. The regrets would be theirs
alone later on.

"Just asking," Joe said.

"Is there anything more for us to do?" Kramer asked.

"One thing," Joe told him. "Let's roll on out."

"Aren't you going to . . . you know . . . make some an-
nouncement? Or something? Something a little dramatic
maybe?"

"Nope. The road's plain enough. I expect do you get

your wagon on it, I can convince the others to go along with you. So whyn't you roll, Samuel. It's time to go t' California."

Kramer took a deep breath and hesitated for a very brief moment. Joe could only imagine what thoughts the man must be having, leaving behind everything and everyone he knew, heading out into a strange and sometimes hostile land. But he was game. They all were. They had to be, else they would not be here ready to start off on an adventure into a new life.

"Tommy. Let's go now."

"Do you mean it, Papa? We should go?"

"I said so, didn't I? Start them off now, boy. Let's go to Californy."

The boy—Joe guessed him to be fourteen or thereabouts—grinned and turned to prod the near leader. "Hyah, Bob. Hup, Bill."

Slowly, ponderously, the six oxen leaned into their yokes and began to pull. Kramer's big Studebaker commenced to roll forward at a walking pace.

"One step at a time," Joe reminded the Kramers. And everyone else within hearing. "That's all it takes is one step at a time."

The wagons strung out for a mile and a half or perhaps more. There was no particular order of travel. Each wagon was welcome to go more or less as they pleased. Here and there, a large family or a group of friends traveling in more than one wagon moved close together. Sometimes, there could be a gap of thirty or forty yards from one wagon to the next.

This early in the season, with the grass growing thick and with dew on the ground to provide a little moisture, there was no dust to contend with. Later, when civilization was months behind them, these green emigrants would know what heat and dust were. Likely, they would know loneliness and fear as well.

Joe had told them. Warned them. He did not want any one of them to be able to accuse him later of failing to prepare them for the ordeals of the road.

He knew a good many of them, perhaps even most, would think he was exaggerating. Soon enough, they would know he told them no more than an unvarnished truth.

That was the way of things, though. No lesson is so well learned as the one driven home by experience.

Joe let the Kramer family lead the way while he and the red-and-white paint roved back and forth through the mass of wagons, encouraging them to follow.

In general, the menfolk walked with their oxen while the women rode in the wagons and the children played close to their family's wagon, running and yipping in childish imitation of Indian war cries. Within a few days, the children would be riding inside the wagons too. And within a few months, the women and the stronger children would be walking alongside in order to preserve the strength of their teams. That was the time when Joe predicted he would see Mrs. Hallett's fine chiffonier set with loving care and genuine regret at the side of the road in the hope they might someday come back for it—they would not—or at the least that someone would find and value it. And that was as little likely as the Halletts returning two thousand miles just for a piece of furniture.

Joe pulled the paint over to one side and sat for a few minutes watching. He was pleased with what he saw. Most of these people were fairly well off. There were a few rigs being pulled by four oxen, but most of the wagons were drawn by sixes for an extra margin of safety. By the time they reached the end of this long road, very few would have their original complement of oxen.

And some wagons probably would not make it as far as California. Some would turn back. Some would settle for Colorado Territory or for the vast emptiness of Wyoming.

Today, though, today all was hope and smiles and excitement, with no thought of failure.

"Come along, Adam. You keep fooling with your outfit like that you won't ever get under way."

"My damn chains is tangled," the emigrant said unhappily. He was bent over a pile of chain while his four oxen and secondhand wagon stood motionless. Adam Sparks seemed destined to be the last man in the train. Not that there was anything wrong with that. Someone had to be.

"Like I told everybody at the meeting the other night," Joe said, very much aware that Sparks had not attended that gathering, "every night before you sleep you want to get your traces sorted ready for use. Sometimes you'll have to yoke up in pitch-black night, and you want everything to hand when that time comes."

"I'll remember you said that, Mr. Moss."

Joe doubted that, but it was only fair to give Sparks the benefit of the doubt. Plenty of doubt remained, though, even after Joe marked off that proverbial "benefit."

"Whenever you're ready, Adam, we'll be over yonder way." Joe touched the brim of his hat to Mrs. Sparks and gigged the paint into motion again to catch up with the others who were toiling on ahead.

Be damned, he thought. Even *I'm* kinda excited t' be on the road again. See some real country. Eat some liver still warm from the kill.

He smiled as he took the paint forward.

✢ 3 ✢

JOE FILLED HIS coffee cup and carried it outside the ring of overly bright firelight. He could never get used to the way these green emigrants built their fires. Five times bigger than was needed and using ten times as much fuel. That was bad enough, but the big fires could be all too easily seen from afar, and when a man stood close to one, his night vision was ruined.

Not that there were any enemies about. Not this close to civilization. But even so. A man doesn't want to become sloppy in his habits. And they would not always be in tame surroundings.

He went far enough that he could see the stars again and listen to the distant sounds of the night cutting through the drone of talk behind him and the clatter of tinware as the people finished their dinners.

Joe walked to the edge of the encampment and lifted his face to the sky and opened his nostrils to the breeze. The smells of the train—livestock and wood smoke and boiling foods—were behind him. Here he could smell the grass, lush and laden with moisture now. The earth, sunbaked and drying. And somewhere far away, the faint scent of rain. Within a day or two, he thought, they would be traveling in the wet. That, with a little mud on the ground, was when they would learn who was too heavily loaded and who had been sensible enough to pare down to the necessities.

He heard a footfall behind him and whirled, his hand by habit going to the hilt of his knife. The girl who stood there did not notice that. It took Joe a moment to remember who this one was. She was Wilcox's daughter Harriet, thirteen or fourteen, he judged, and in truth more than a little on the homely side of things.

"Good evening, miss." He removed his wide-brimmed hat and held it at his side. The girl was flustered, and for a moment was tongue-tied. Likely, she was not yet accustomed to having grown men treat her like a lady.

"I . . . I . . . my mama wants me to ask you something, Mr. Moss, sir."

"You're welcome to ask it, missy, but my name is Joe to my friends. You can call me that if you've a mind to."

"Yes, sir." She looked like she was ready to bolt back toward her family's fire if he so much as raised his hand to scratch an itch.

Joe waited. After a moment of awkward silence, he prompted, "You have a question?"

"My . . . my mama does, yes, sir." Suggesting that Harriet did not at all want to be here but her mama wanted to initiate a conversation between the girl and Moss. He smiled a little. Matchmaking this early in the trip? Mrs. Wilcox was a woman who did not believe in waiting until the last minute for things. Before they reached California, half the marriageable girls in the train would have crushes on him—he knew that—and the mothers of the other half would be thinking of him as a mighty eligible bachelor.

"So what would that question be, missy?"

"I . . . she . . . was wondering . . . how far we've come now."

He almost broke out laughing. On the road for seventeen days and someone was already fretting about the distance? He certainly hoped this was just the woman's ploy to put her daughter under his nose and not a genuine concern with the travel, or Mrs. Wilcox would be plenty unhappy before they crossed the Sierras.

"You can tell her we've come about a hundred fifty miles, child, or perhaps a trifle more. Tell her that, oh, day after tomorrow, I think, we'll be getting to a nice little grove inside a bend of the river. We'll stop there for a day so's people can mend their gear and wash clothes, tend to the little things they've learned about being on the road and like that. Then we'll get down to traveling in earnest."

The girl appeared to relax just a little. "Mr. Moss . . ."

"Joe," he corrected.

"Yes, sir. Can I ask you something?"

"Of course."

"Are there"—she looked around rather apprehensively—"are there . . . you know."

"Wild Indians?" he guessed.

"Yes, sir."

"Not around here. Any Injuns we see this close in will be friendly. Later on, we'll see plenty of Indians."

"Wild ones?"

"Not so wild as you might think, but yes. They'll be what you would call wild Indians."

"Will they . . . um . . ."

"No," he said quickly. "I won't let there be any trouble."

"But how . . . that is . . . ?"

"I know the tribes we're likely to run into along this route.

I get along with them just fine. I've trapped in the mountains out there, and I've traded with the Indians. Lived with them over the winters for more than a dozen years. I know them, and they know me. I won't let there be any trouble, Harriet."

"You know my name?" She sounded pleased.

"Yes, of course."

The homely child smiled a little. "You really think we'll be safe from the Indians, Mr. Moss?"

"I'm sure of it. We'll be in danger from heat and thirst and mosquitoes and chiggers and maybe even hunger. We aren't likely to have any worries about wild Indians, though." That was true enough. Mostly. And any exceptions were not something he would want to burden this young girl with. If it came time to worry, he would let her and the others know about it then. With any kind of luck, though, what he'd told her was the whole truth. But then, dealing with that sort of thing was why he'd been hired to shepherd these folks west.

"Thank you, Mr. Moss. I feel better now."

"Then I'm very glad your mama sent you over to ask that question."

"The day after tomorrow, you said?"

"That's right. We should get to the grove early in the day and have a little time to make any final adjustments before we get serious about this traveling."

Harriet grinned. Her chin came up and she no longer stood there flat-footed and slouching. "Can I tell everybody?"

"Sure. You take the news to them for me, will you?"

"Yes, sir." She gave a little yip and went racing off toward the wagons.

Joe turned back to the breeze and the stars. It was good out here, he thought. Mighty good.

✢ 4 ✢

THEY ROLLED INTO the grove late in the forenoon. Joe could as good as feel the sense of excitement running through the train. The people were eager for the layover. Joe sat on his paint beside the line of march so that each wagon had to pass by him on its way in to choose a spot to camp. He eyed the wagons and the livestock—and the people—as each came by.

"Your off swing ox is favoring his left hind foot there, mister. You might ought to take a look, see if he has a pebble lodged or a stone bruise."

"Did you notice the tire on that wheel, James? It's starting to work loose. Better you should take that wheel over to Aaron, I think, an' let him reset the tire before you have a problem on your hands."

"Mornin', Miz Blaylock. Boys." Joe smiled and touched the brim of his hat.

A few rigs further he said, "Howdy, Samuel. Fine day, isn't it? I tell you what you can do if you would. You might want t' pass the word around for all the menfolk to gather this evening after supper. I know there's prob'ly questions by now and problems folks will want t' bring up. This will be a good time t' get them out to where we can have a look at them." He took his hat off and wiped a trickle of sweat out of his eyes, then added, "After the meeting we'll play a little music, them as care to, and maybe dance a little too. *Dammit!*"

Joe jumped the paint into a sudden lunge and raised up in his stirrups as he tore across the grove to the riverbank. "Damn you, Thompson, don't you have the least lick of sense? Take them oxes over t' the downstream side before you water them. Ain't nobody on this train wants to drink piss and slobber in with his coffee. And don't let me see you getting lazy about this again neither. D'you hear me, mister?"

"Yes, sir, I hear you."

Still scowling, Joe walked his horse hock-deep into the water and let it drink before he reined away. Ed Thompson did not say a word about this obvious and quite deliberate inequity.

The wagons of the train trickled in for more than an hour. The smell of wood smoke soon filled the grove along with the scents of fresh manure and cooking foods. Joe rode through the sprawling encampment, directing the livestock to a flat on the downstream edge of the grove and designating the families with middlin'-age boys who could be pressed into service as herders.

When he was satisfied that the camp was settling in well enough, he rode to the back of the light trailer Sam Kramer pulled behind his wagon. Joe kept his bedroll and a pair of parfleche containers there. He generally slept in the open a little apart from the train. He was simply more comfortable that way. He took his meals with Kramer or one of the other emigration company officers; that was part of his deal when he agreed to guide and manage the train for them.

He lifted the paint into a lope, rode two hundred yards or so upstream from the grove, and dropped his bedroll beside the river, dismounted, and hobbled the horse, then turned it loose so it could fill its belly with the lush new grass.

Joe cast a baleful eye toward the sky. It wouldn't be long, he figured, before the rain came.

But then, if a man objected to getting a little wet, he had no business living and working in the open. Better he should huddle inside one of those tall buildings in the cities. Joe once saw a hotel that went four floors up from the ground. Just looking at the damn thing had made him nervous and there was no way he would have set foot inside. Why, if those flimsy walls gave way . . . it was just plain unnatural to pile bricks and timbers that high. It couldn't possibly be safe.

Satisfied, Joe turned and began walking back toward the grove where the emigrants were gathered loudly reveling in this break from the routines of travel.

Joe scowled at the thin haze of dust hanging in the air along their back trail. If the sun had not been slanting so low at this time of day, even his practiced eyes might have missed it.

But then he knew by now to watch for it. Someone was following them, had been since they pulled out of St. Jo. Followed them along the north fork of the creek Joe knew as the Kinikinick, now across to the south bank of the Little Blue. Whoever it was, this was a free country. They were entitled to go where they wished. Including out on the open prairie without the presence of other folks in an emigrant train for mutual protection if that was what they really wanted to do.

Several times early in the journey, he'd dropped back behind Sam Kramer's company far enough to ascertain that it was only one wagon following, a six-ox hitch pulling a canvas-covered wagon with no trailer and no livestock other than the oxen. He hadn't bothered to get in close to the parasite, but it was easy enough to see that the wagon seemed to be occupied by two women, one of whom rode the lazyboard while the other handled the oxen. Every few miles, the two would switch off their duties, the one in the pale blue dress taking over from the taller one in the gray and then vice versa.

He'd tried several times to puzzle out why two women traveling alone would hang back like that. The best answer he could come up with was that they were too poor to pay the fee required to sign the emigrant company's articles and become an official member of the train.

Not that it was any of his never-mind. He told himself that again.

But maybe tomorrow, he would ride down to their camp and make their acquaintance.

After all, if something happened to them, he would hold himself responsible if the only thing holding them apart was a lack of wherewithal. If that was the case, perhaps he could have a word with Kramer and the company directors about allowing them to pull their wagon in with the others.

Not that he really expected any trouble. He'd told Wilcox's daughter the truth about that. He figured he could take care of any Indians without resorting to violence on either side. But there were all manner of dangers on a venture like this one, and hostile human beings could be the very least of those. A couple women traveling alone likely would not know how to cope with broken axles or thrown tires, a broke-leg ox or a leaking water barrel.

He glanced at the sky to the west, where a line of gray rimmed the horizon. Hell, those women back there might not even know to stay out of the low places when rain came.

He'd seen more than one wagon full of pilgrims get swept away in a flash flood after they were damn fool enough to make camp in a dry wash. How people like that thought those washes came to be if not carved by fast-running water, he never could understand. They simply didn't think at all was all he could figure. Just plain did not think things through.

Tonight if he had time, or tomorrow morning for certain sure, he decided, he would go back and talk to those women and see if they knew what they were doing.

Pleased now that he'd worked out what he intended to do about the tail on this dog, he headed for Kramer's wagon, his mouth watering and belly growling in anticipation of Mrs. Kramer's good cooking. With any kind of luck, he was thinking, he might be able to knock down a prairie chicken or two when he went to talk to those women.

It would make the visit all the more worthwhile if he could bring meat back.

✦ 5 ✦

IT WOULD SOON be dark. The folks were finished with their suppers, or at least most of them were, and the older boys had gathered enough wood for the council fire to keep it blazing for the next week. Or, the way these emigrants built their fires, for the next several hours anyway.

The people were beginning to gather around the fire where Joe proposed to go over the rules again—some were becoming lax already—and try to impress upon them just how far they had to go. These people were still green as new grass, never mind that they were thinking of themselves as seasoned travelers.

All in all, though, things were going well enough. He was satisfied. He stood in the cool, evening air enjoying the slow drift of the river—it would have been considered nothing more than a creek back East, but here it counted as a river—and the sounds of a pack of children who were fretting their mamas with their splashing and general tomfoolery. He liked the sound of children at play. It gave a man a sense of contentment, never mind were the children boys or girls, white or red.

Joe opened his possibles pouch and fetched out his pipe and a plug of tobacco, then used his knife to slice off a bit of the hard-packed tobacco that he crumbled and carefully tamped in the bowl of the pipe. He bent to gather a few sprigs of last season's dry grass, intending to twist the stems together and borrow a little flame from the council fire for his pipe. He did not finish the task, however. Someone was coming up the riverbank. Someone on foot.

Joe had left his rifle at Kramer's wagon. Now he regretted that. He lightly touched the butts of the two pistols in his sash and the iron head of the tomahawk at his waist.

There were—he squinted into the gloom of the evening—two people.

Those women, he realized, the ones who had been following the train. He'd intended to go speak with them in the morning anyway. Now it looked like they were going to save him the trouble.

He dropped the pipe back into his possibles bag and walked down to meet them.

The twilight was rapidly fading away, so for the most part the women were a pair of shapes without color or detail, one somewhat taller than the other.

Joe removed his wide-brimmed Mexican hat and nodded. "Evenin', ladies." He introduced himself. "What can I do for you folks?"

"I am Margaret McCarthy," the shorter woman said. "This is my daughter Fiona. We . . . we have been following along behind the train for some days now."

"Yes, ma'am, Miz McCarthy. I knew you were back there. Are you having trouble?"

"Not exactly, Mr. Moss. We want to rejoin the company."

"Rejoin, ma'am?" Joe was certain he had never seen either of these women before.

"We are fully paid-up members of the company, Mr. Moss. We want to return to the train now."

"Well, ma'am, if you're already members o' the company, I don't see why the officers would object to havin' you take your place with the rest."

"What my mother has neglected to mention, Mr. Moss, is that we were evicted from the train." The daughter's voice was pleasant. Soft and gentle.

"Why, Miss McCarthy, I'm real sorry t' hear that, but I'd be glad to have a word with Kramer and the other officers about lettin' you folks back in. I don't know what his reasons was nor if he's set on sticking by them, but I'll talk to him. I can promise you that much."

"It was not Mr. Kramer or the officers who sent us away to fend for ourselves against wild Indians and God knows what else, Mr. Moss."

"I'm afraid I don't understand. If it wasn't Kramer and the board, then who was it had that kind of say-so?"

"You did it, Mr. Moss," the girl said softly, her voice more sad than accusing.

"Me?" Joe blurted out. "Why, I never—"

"It was on account of my father, Mr. Moss."

"I don't recall . . . oh, maybe I do at that. Big man? Got some gray in his beard?"

"My husband is a good man, Mr. Moss," the older woman said. "He has a temper. I do not dispute that. But he is a good man. Really he is. And we . . . Mr. Moss, we invested everything we had, what little there was of it, in this opportunity to make a new start in California. We haven't any money to pay our way into another company. And we can't turn around and go back. That would humiliate him,

Mr. Moss, and Brendan is a man who cannot take humiliation. He has his pride. Failure now, not even getting a good start on the journey, it would kill him. I just know it would."

As Joe recalled, McCarthy had been damn well humiliated back there in St. Jo, down on his knees and scared to pick up his knife, with half the menfolk in the train seeing it happen. Yeah, Joe would call that a humiliating sort of experience. Apparently, the son of a bitch hadn't mentioned that little detail to his wife or his daughter.

"Where is your husband now, Miz McCarthy? I've seen you ladies and your wagon, but I never saw Mr. McCarthy."

"My husband is . . . indisposed, Mr. Moss. Temporarily."

"Let me ask you somethin' straight out then, ma'am. Is your husband laying up drunk?"

Mrs. McCarthy did not answer, but Fiona did. She squared her shoulders and held her chin high. "Yes, he is, Mr. Moss."

"He do this sort o' thing often, does he?"

"No. Not really. Just . . . sometimes."

"Uh-huh."

"Don't you *dare* act so sanctimonious and holier-than-thou." The girl seemed to have her father's temper. "My father is a good man. A better man than you, I'd wager. You have no right to take his dreams away from him. No right to steal his hopes for a better life."

"Did he tell you why I kicked him outa the train, Miss McCarthy?"

"Yes, he did. He got into an argument with Simon Taylor. Something to do with a card game; he did not say exactly what. He said the two of them would have worked it out between them except you came along and took it for something more than it really was."

"Is that so?"

"Yes, Mr. Moss, that is so. You were entirely too quick to throw your weight around. You bullied my father. You threatened him with a gun. Do you deny that? Do you?"

Joe fingered his chin for a moment. "No, I reckon you could look at it like that."

"You did threaten him with a gun, didn't you?"

"It wasn't no threat, miss. I meant every word I said to the man. I would've shot him dead, and I expect he knew that."

Mrs. McCarthy gasped. Fiona just got all the more angry. "You are a very unpleasant man, Mr. Moss."

"Yes, miss, I expect that's prob'ly true."

"I demand that you allow us to rejoin this wagon train. If you don't, I will . . . I will . . ." She stamped her foot in frustration and fury. "I don't know what I will do. But you would regret it. I promise you that, sir."

"Your pa is a drunk with a bad temper, miss. We don't need none of that in such a small company travelin' close together for so very long."

"He is not a drunk."

"We are out of liquor now anyway, Mr. Moss," the mother put in. "He has already finished everything we laid by for the trip. And he will be on his best behavior. I promise you that. No more drinking. And he will keep a tight rein on his temper."

"We have no choice but to go on, Mr. Moss," the girl said. "Will you make us do it alone? Will you endanger our very lives just because you and my father got off to a . . . a bad start? Can you not find it in your heart to relent and give us another chance?"

Us, she'd said. And of course she was right. In sending Brendan McCarthy out of the train, Joe might have doomed the man's wife and daughter as well.

It was one thing to face the father. Hell, given cause, Joe

would cut the man's heart out and leave his corpse for the crows without a single qualm.

But it was another thing entire to bring harm to a couple women who had the misfortune of being related to a son of a bitch like Brendan McCarthy.

"Please?" The girl's voice was soft again, gentle, her anger apparently having flown as quickly as it rose.

"We'll not give you any trouble," Mrs. McCarthy pledged. "Not the least bit."

Joe sighed. He couldn't see that he had much choice about it. "All right," he said. "Tomorrow morning you can pull your wagon in with the rest. We'll be laying over here for another full day at the least, so you can wash clothes or do whatever it is that needs doing."

Things like getting Brendan McCarthy sobered up and standing on his own hind legs again, Joe thought. But he did not say anything. That would just be rubbing the women's noses in it, and they had done nothing to deserve that.

"Thank you, Mr. Moss. You will not regret this. I promise."

"Yes, ma'am." He hoped the woman was right about that, never mind any reservations he might have about the whole thing.

Joe put his hat back on and touched the brim politely, then bowed his way away and headed to the bonfire where the emigrants were waiting for him.

✦ 6 ✦

I T WAS LATE in the afternoon the following day when the McCarthy wagon pulled in to join the others. Joe watched from a distance as a flock of women from the other wagons came rushing to greet the McCarthys. So Mrs. McCarthy and the daughter were popular with the other ladies on the train. There was no such round of greetings from the menfolk, however, and Joe still did not see Brendan outside and upright. The two women, mostly the taller one in the gray dress, had to do all the work of unyoking the oxen and setting up their camp. Joe recalled from last night that the daughter was the taller. What was her name again? It took him a moment to recall it. Fiona, that was it. He'd known a woman named Fiona once before. But, he thought with a grin, maybe that acquaintance didn't count. That Fiona had been a plump and bouncy little whore up in Astoria. That one knew how to treat a man, though. She surely did.

His grin became wider as he remembered the Oregon Fiona. She'd been fun, she had. He'd laid up with her for two days, and would have stayed longer except she mistook his bullet pouch for a bag of gold nuggets and took off with it, which made his time with her a grand bargain. Even cheaper than he could have gotten an Indian girl, so the joke was on her. And right up until then—Joe rolled his eyes— yeah, that Fiona had definitely given him a good time.

Not that he was making any comparisons. Just remembering, that was all. He rolled his eyes again and turned away from watching the ladies of the train flock around the McCarthy women a hundred fifty yards or so distant.

He wandered among the wagons, looking to see that things were all right with each of them. There had been little time for these wagons to begin deteriorating, but a wagon is like a fence. Turn your back on it for more than a couple minutes and it will start falling apart. A man had to keep after them if he intended to keep them.

"Afternoon, Miz Clayborne, Billy." He touched his hat and moved along.

A few wagons further he reminded the owner, "I see your water barrel isn't full, Benson. Don't forget to top it off this afternoon. There won't be time to do it in the morning, an' we'll be leaving the river now an' cutting across to the Platte. It will be a spell before we see live water again so fill up while you can."

Some of the men had set up a folding camp table like those favored by Army officers—useless, self-indulgent assholes for the most part, he thought; the officers, that is, not these emigrants—and were playing a card game, one that Joe did not recognize even though there were wagers involved. It looked complicated. Joe liked gambling plenty well enough, but was content with simple games. Like the Indian game of Hand, where all you had to do was figure out in which hand the other man was holding a pebble. The odds were even in that one, and the real contest lay in one man's ability to cut through the deliberate deceptions and read the mind and the intentions of the other fellow. Joe liked to play Hand. So much so that he didn't even cheat when he played it.

He wandered along inside the camp for a little while, then decided to take some of his own advice and take advantage of this water and the layover while he could. He walked upstream to his camp and stripped off the doeskin hunting shirt, exposing a body that was marked with old scars. He'd been shot, stabbed, and hit by hostile arrows, and he would carry the tracks of his past on his pelt to the end of his days. Not that he had any regrets. After all, he was still upright on his own hind legs. The enemies he'd left behind while getting these scars were not.

They hadn't been on the road all that long and the shirt was fairly fresh and free of lice. Eventually, he would have to hunt up an anthill to lay the garment out on for the ants to clean off the lice and nits, but right now that didn't seem necessary.

He kicked off his moccasins and laid his weapons, sash, and other gear aside, then shucked out of his trousers and tossed them into the slowly moving water. Quickly, he bent to retrieve his tomahawk and followed the britches into the river. The trousers could use washing, and the side of the tomahawk served nicely to beat his laundry. And having it in hand kept him from being defenseless while he was bathing.

Not that he expected trouble in this close to civilization, but old habits—the good ones especially—die hard.

Joe hummed softly to himself, although the actual sound was more a series of grunts and snorts than an identifiable tune. The words, had he sung them aloud, were a Lakota chant that celebrated a successful hunt. Not that Joe's hunts were always successful. But he always expected them to be.

He sat cross-legged in the river, the cool, swirling water coming to his waist as he did so. His trousers lay over his lap as, over and over, he dipped them into the stream, then lifted them out to wring them as dry as he could get them before plunging them back into the water. He had already spent considerable time beating the pants with the flat of his tomahawk, and now the rinse water was nice and clear and free of the muddy brown sludge that seeped out of the cloth when he began.

He felt good. Content. The sun lay warm on his skin and he felt fresh, clean, and at least for the moment free of danger or care. For now, he was not even carrying the burdens of the emigrant train. Tomorrow would be quite soon enough to worry about that.

He gave the trousers a hard twist, cords of ropy muscle standing out on his forearms, and brought the chant inside his head to an agreeable halt. A good hunt. Aye, he remembered some very good hunts. In a month or so, they should be seeing buffalo and he could lay in some meat for the emigrants. He—

"Mr. Moss."

Joe lunged to his feet, tomahawk instinctively raised ready to slash or to throw. He was already upright before it registered that that voice had been soft and female and . . .

Female!

Good God.

Joe's trousers trailed limply from his left hand while his right brandished the tomahawk. He stood in the river naked as the day he was born.

On the bank a few paces distant was a girl. A pretty girl. Maybe, dammit, the prettiest girl he had ever seen.

And he was . . .

"Oh, shit." He snatched the trousers front and center to cover himself as best he was able, and immediately plopped back down into the river. Reconsidered how rude that would seem, and jumped up again. Tried to cover himself. Yearned desperately for a hole he could crawl into or for a bolt of lightning to strike him dead on the spot. "Shit," he repeated, rather more loudly than might have been necessary.

The girl, damn her, stood there laughing.

"I am sorry, Mr. Moss. I am so very sorry. I didn't mean to creep up on you like that."

"I'm the one that's sorry, Miss . . . you are Miss McCarthy, aren't you? It was dark last night and I didn't get a proper look at you."

Most especially, the night before he hadn't been able to see the vivid red of her hair nor the spray of freckles on her nose and cheeks nor the softness of her skin, the delicate column of her neck, and the tender throat—he had a sudden desire to touch her neck, to kiss that softly pulsing spot on her throat—nor had he really appreciated how slim she was. She was as slender as a sword blade. She . . .

Joe shook himself and hurriedly pulled his shirt over his head. He'd already stepped into his trousers—while he was still sitting in the all-too-shallow river—and his moccasins. He felt considerably better once he had his shirt on too. He bent down for his sash and accoutrements and rather gruffly stuffed the pistols, knife, and tomahawk back where they belonged, back where he could be comfortable knowing they were at hand. Finally, he slung the pouches over his shoulders, one crisscrossing from the left shoulder and the other from his right.

He had been avoiding looking at the girl for fear he would end up staring. Now he let his eyes meet hers. They were . . . green? Almost. And with flecks of gold. He shivered, trying to shake off whatever it was about this girl that made him feel awkward and oafish. And old. He was old enough to be her father; he was sure of it. But there was something about her . . .

"What can I do for you, Miss McCarthy?"

"My name is Fiona, sir."

"All right. Fiona."

"And the reason I walked up here was to thank you. For allowing us to rejoin the wagon train, I mean. It means a lot. To all of us."

"I just"—he shrugged—"just tryin' to do what's right. D'you understand?"

"Yes, I think I do. Papa can be . . . he can be a very difficult man. I know that. But he is a good husband to my mother and a good father to me. He means no harm, Mr. Moss. Really he doesn't."

It occurred to him that there was no hint of brogue in her voice, and he suspected that despite the Irish name she had been raised in this country.

It also occurred to him that he felt a desire to know this girl, to know everything about her. Where she came from. What she hoped for and dreamt of. What she felt and thought and . . . everything.

Joe felt heat in his cheeks. He cleared his throat and bent down to retrieve the rifle that he'd leaned against the Mexican saddle that served as both pillow and backrest when he laid out his camp each night.

She glanced at the rifle and quickly said, "I don't mean to keep you from your work. I just wanted to thank you. Going West means the world to Papa."

"But not to you," he guessed, "or to your mama?"

"Papa decides these things. We do whatever he wants."

"What is it that you want, Miss McCarthy? Fiona?"

"It isn't important what I want, Mr. Moss. I am but a woman. And a spinster woman at that." Fiona smiled, and for Joe the sun beamed brighter because of it.

"A spinster lady, is it?"

"Aye, sir. Twenty and two years of age and nary a suitor in sight." She was still smiling, but Joe got the impression there was a sadness lying behind those words. And in truth, it was unusual indeed for a young woman to reach such an age, especially a pretty woman, yet remain unmarried.

"Your father," he said, his voice gently inquiring. "He does not approve of the young dandies who would court his daughter?"

"He . . ." Fiona snapped her mouth shut and suddenly frowned. "I did not come here to complain, sir, nor to tell you my troubles. Should I have any troubles, which I firmly deny. I only came to thank you, and having done that, I ask permission, sir, to take my leave now if you please."

If he pleased? He did *not* please. What he pleased would be for Fiona McCarthy to sit beside him here on the river-bank and tell him every thought she ever had and every dream she hoped to have. What he pleased would be to know her, really know her. And to touch her. Not to hurt her nor to compromise her. Just to touch her. To know the feel of her skin. To know her scent. To know . . .

"Wait a moment, please. Don't move."

"What's wrong?" Fiona asked.

"Shh. Don't move." Joe stepped close to her and leaned down. He lightly pinched the cloth of her dress below her knee, then snapped his hand away shaking it and muttering a little.

"What is it?"

"Nothing now. A bug. I didn't want it to sting you."

"Oh. Well . . . thank you."

"You're welcome." There had been no bug. But now he knew that Fiona smelled of soap and yeast and a delicately heady scent of her own, light and indefinable and intoxicating.

The girl's face flushed red and he wondered if she had guessed his ruse. He felt an impulse to apologize, but to do that he would have to admit what he had done, and he did not want to do that.

"I . . . I have to go now, Mr. Moss."

"Joe," he said. "My name is Joe."

"Yes, I . . . I have to go now." She seemed flustered. Upset.

Joe quickly stepped back away from her. He did not want to frighten her. Hardly. He wanted to protect her. From every sort of hurt.

"Good-bye, Mr. Moss."

"Good-bye, Miss McCarthy."

But neither turned away.

They stood. Only a few feet apart. Eyes meeting. Wordless and unmoving.

After a brief moment that felt as if long minutes had passed, Fiona blinked. She turned. She gathered her skirts in her hands and ran back toward the wagon encampment while Joe stood watching every step she took until she was within the grove and lost to his sight.

THE FIREWOOD THEY gathered last night was nothing compared with what they'd pulled together this evening. Emigrants! Joe shook his head, although in amusement rather than censure.

It was fine, though. Come morning they would be back to the dust and the heat and the toil of travel. Tonight, they could relax. Talk and gossip. Those that had them would likely bring out their musical instruments. Probably some of them would sing and others dance. There was no harm in any of it. Joe leaned against the trunk of a gnarled tree and enjoyed the sounds and the sights that swirled about him as the emigrants left their suppers and drifted toward the clearing where the makings of their huge bonfire were laid.

"Good evening, Mr. Moss."

"Good evening, dearie." He could not remember the little girl's name. She was nine or maybe ten years old and had pigtails and a permanent smile beneath the brim of her oversized bonnet. She was with Mr. and Mrs. Parker's wagon, but he seemed to recall the child was not a Parker. Could be Mrs. Parker had been a widow who had the little girl and then remarried, or there could be some other explanation. Joe hadn't asked and hadn't been told. It didn't matter. The child was sweet and gave Joe a wide smile when she passed by.

He could see a knot of men gathered by the river. Brendan McCarthy was with them. Simon Taylor, the man McCarthy had an altercation with when Joe first joined the train, was not. Either Brendan had not seen Joe or was ignoring him. Either was perfectly acceptable so far as Joe was concerned.

A boy in his teens came running from the direction of the open prairie. "Riders coming," he was hollering. "There's a pack train coming in."

That got the attention of the menfolk. Got Joe's attention too. He drifted along behind the others as they set out in the direction the boy indicated.

There were three riders along with a short string of pack mules, he saw when he got clear of the trees. The men all wore the wide-brimmed Mexican hats similar to Joe's, the very practical sort favored by traders and trappers and other men of the mountains. As they came near, he recognized the one in the lead. "Aw, shit," he said to no one in particular.

"Is that you, Moss?"

"It's me all right, Tharp. And it's your hard luck that you run into me here."

"I don't want no trouble with you, Moss." The man named Tharp drew rein at the edge of the grove and slid out of his saddle. The two who were with him remained mounted.

Joe ignored Tharp. He walked over to the lead mule and laid a hand on one of the three kegs loaded onto the pack-saddle. There were six mules in the string and five of them were carrying the same load. Joe had no trouble figuring out what would be in those kegs.

"You can leave be, Moss. I'm going out to trade with the Injuns nice and peaceable."

"You're carrying liquid death there, Tharp, and you know it. Is it even potable alcohol? D'you even care?"

"I didn't know it was wood alcohol that time, Moss. Some slick sharper in St. Louis sold it to me. I didn't know."

The man's rotgut two years earlier had killed at least four Cheyenne that Joe knew of, and there may have been more that he hadn't heard about.

"I didn't believe you then, Tharp, and I don't believe you now."

"Is there trouble, Mr. Moss?" Samuel Kramer asked, joining them. Joe explained, loudly enough for all to hear.

"Tharp here is a liar and a cheat and a murderer."

"Damn you, Moss, you can't accuse me o' that."

"I just did, you son of a bitch. You're all of those things and a hell of a lot more. And I'll tell you something else. You aren't taking any of this one step further. I won't have you using it to kill innocent folk."

"Innocent? They're nothing but a bunch of stinking savages an' you know it."

"If you feel that way about them, Tharp, you got no business trading with them. They're folks. They got different ways than us but they're people just the same, and I'm not gonna see you take this alcohol out so's you can rob and kill them."

"You got nothing to say about it, Moss. You can't tell me shit."

Joe grunted. He pulled the tomahawk from his belt and used it to knock the bung out of the nearest keg. Alcohol, colorless but slightly clouded with impurities, began pouring onto the mule's side and running down its leg onto the ground.

"Hey! Damn you, Moss. You can't . . ."

Joe swung the tomahawk again and the topmost keg began draining whiskey onto the mule's sweaty back. The animal shied and began to fidget.

Tharp swung about in his saddle to bring the muzzle of his rifle on line, hauling the hammer back to full cock as he did so.

Before Tharp could shoot, Joe stepped in close. He pushed the rifle barrel aside and yanked the weapon out of Tharp's hands. Tharp's finger was already on the trigger and the rifle discharged, the muzzle flame singeing Joe's upper arm, but the ball passing by without touching him.

Tharp spilled out of his saddle and fell heavily to the ground, losing his grip on the empty rifle. The man rolled under the belly of his horse and came to his feet on the other side of it.

"This time, Moss, I'm going to kill you," Tharp shouted as he pulled a long, double-edged knife from a sheath on his belt. "I'm going to cut you up one side an' down the other, damn you."

Joe Moss said nothing, just released his hold on Tharp's rifle and let it fall with a loud clatter onto the ground. With his left hand, he drew the bowie from the sheath in his sash. The tomahawk was still in his right.

Tharp grimaced, then bent low and let out a loud roar.

"You fixin' to bite me, Tharp, or d'you intend t' use that pig-sticker?"

"Kill you is what I'm gonna do, Moss. I'm gonna kill you dead."

"If you can, you sonuvabitch," Joe responded. He stood waiting for Tharp's charge, the steel of the bowie weaving back and forth like a snake's head, the tomahawk held low at his right hip.

Tharp's eyes were locked on the deadly dance of the bowie knife and he crabbed slightly to his left, toward Joe's right, obviously intending to remain as far away as he could get from the slashing range of that knife. He held his own Arkansas knife out before him, his left hand and forearm poised protectively above it ready to intercept any move Joe might make. It seemed clear that fighting with knives was something the man had experience with.

Both men were bent forward at the waist so the soft and vulnerable tissue of their bellies was as far from danger as it was possible to hold it.

Joe was content to let Tharp make the first move. And one was all there was likely to be. One sudden, vicious lunge, one flurry of motion with hand and steel, and it would be ended. A knife fight generally lasts little longer than a heartbeat unless the two combatants are exceptionally well matched. And Joe did not believe that Tharp was any match for him.

If the truth were known, Joe did not believe there was any other man—not on the plains nor in the mountains—who was his equal in a fight. And he had yet to be proven wrong about that.

The dance leading up to the furious and deadly clash, however, could be lengthy indeed. Joe was patient, though. He did not intend to rush this. Tharp could take all the time he wanted, circling and shuffling, his upper body leaning forward and bobbing up and down like some oversized fighting cock, his lip curled into a wicked snarl while low growling noises issued from his throat. It was all intended to intimidate.

Joe waited. Waited.

Tharp quit circling to Joe's right and half-turned as if to

give up the fight. Inwardly Joe smiled, believing this dance was about to end. He hunched his shoulders and braced himself.

Tharp turned suddenly and came at Joe with an earsplitting screech like the howl of a panther.

Joe flicked the bowie upward and took a half step to his left. Tharp barreled in, knife slashing wickedly, confident in the kill.

Except it was Joe's tomahawk, not the bowie, that met Tharp's charge, the blade of the tomahawk battering down Tharp's guard and landing hard on his knife hand.

Tharp grunted and drew back. He looked down and seemed amazed to discover he no longer held the long Arkansas knife. The bloody weapon lay on the ground between the two men.

For a moment, Tharp stared down at his knife and at the blood that was on it. He peered at Joe, but there was no blood on Joe's belly. Finally Tharp seemed to notice the small, red, sausage-like piece of meat that lay close to his fallen knife.

He looked at it. And then, mutely, at his own right hand. Or what was left of his hand. The thumb that had been wrapped tight around the haft of the Arkansas was . . . gone. It simply was no longer there.

Tharp looked up at Joe again and seemed finally to realize what just happened.

The man tilted his head back and let out a long, quavering scream.

Then again he charged forward. Perhaps intending to batter Joe down with sheer hate. Perhaps with no coherent thought, only an unformed desire to club and to kill.

This time it was Joe's bowie that flashed in the sunlight.

✣ 8 ✣

THEY WERE ALL there, the officers of the emigrant company. Samuel Kramer and Howard Craddock, James Fenn, Luther Sayre, a couple others. They looked like they were going to puke.

Hell, Joe thought, maybe they were. He was positive every man among them had butchered a hog in the past or at least seen one slaughtered. The sight of a hog's guts lying curled in a bucket was not much different from the sight of Tharp's guts lying in a pile on the ground. But these company officers were acting like he'd done something terrible. Joe could not understand that. All he'd done was to defend himself. Tharp might have had a pistol on him or another knife. It would have been stupid for him to stand there waiting to find out. Tharp had already made it clear he wanted to kill Joe. Joe didn't let him. That should have been the end of it.

"My God, man, our women and our children were watching," Fenn grumbled.

Joe looked at him, but still did not say a word. He hadn't

spoken yet, and was not much inclined to do so. He had done nothing wrong, dammit.

"Now looka here, Mr. Moss. We can understand that there was bad blood between you," Martin Lewis said. "You obviously knew each other in the past. That sort of thing happens. He attacked you. There were plenty of witnesses to that. You came out on top. Fine. But . . . dear God . . ." He stopped, apparently too upset to go on.

"I think what Marty is saying, Moss, is that you shouldn't of taken the man's scalp. Especially . . . Good Lord, man, he wasn't even dead yet when you scalped him."

Joe said nothing in response. What the hell was he supposed to say? They were right. Tharp still had been hanging on, sitting on the ground with his lap full of his own guts, trying to stuff the pink and gray coils back inside his belly, when Joe took the son of a bitch's scalp and handed it to the nearer of Tharp's helpers. He'd done it deliberately and for several perfectly good reasons. The first was that it was real likely to discourage the helpers from trying to finish the job their boss couldn't accomplish. The second was to give warning to Tharp's kin. Joe had heard it said that Tharp had family back in Tennessee and that they were a rough bunch. He wanted to make it clear to every one of them that no matter how bad they thought they were, Joe Moss was badder. Meaner, badder, and even more full of piss, so they could stay home in Tennessee or they could come get some of what he gave to their brother or cousin or whatever this Tharp had been to them. Joe'd just wanted to make everything clear, and he reckoned that he had. Maybe these citified folks did not understand that, but Joe was betting that the Tharps would.

"Mr. Moss. Joe. We have been going over this and over it for, what? Twenty minutes? A half hour? And you haven't yet said a word in your own defense," Kramer said. "I wish you would speak up. I really do."

Joe grunted. He kept his silence for a moment longer, then he nodded. "All right, gents. What I will say is this. I'll keep Tharp's stuff, his horse and rifle and like that. I'll use the horse to pack my gear on soon as I can get it out of your trailer, Sam. I'll pull out tomorrow morning or maybe tonight sometime. If you object to that, I can go sooner, but I'd ruther wait until morning if it's all the same to you."

"Wha . . . you would leave us alone out here?"

"Jesus, man, none of us knows the way. We don't know where the water is or how to find game or deal with the red savages or . . ."

Joe gave Luther Sayre a dark look and said, "You want me gone. Isn't that what this is all about? I've offended your women and your kids so you want me gone. Isn't that it?"

"I . . . well, we . . ."

"If you don't want to fire me, why are you wasting my time with this bullshit?" Joe demanded. "Just cut the crap and tell me straight out. Stay or go. It don't make no never-mind to me, but make up your minds an' then leave it be. In or out. I don't care which."

The company officers looked rather nervously from one to another. None of them, he noticed, looked Joe in the eye. The rest of them quickly settled on their president as the focus of their scrutiny.

Sam Kramer cleared his throat and spoke then. "We . . . it is not our intention to send you away, Joseph. We just . . . we thought we should say something, but . . ." His voice tailed away into silence.

"Are you sayin' you want me to stay?" Joe demanded.

"Yes. Of course."

"Then I want you t' say that. Not just you, Sam. I want t' hear it from each man among you. Anybody can't say it right out loud that he wants me t' stay with this train, then I'll be satisfied to leave it tonight."

He waited. And eventually, haltingly, one by one, the company officers stated aloud that they wished for Joe to stay on as their guide and wagon master.

Joe waited until the last of them had spoken, then went to claim the horse and gear that had belonged to the late Mr. Tharp.

✢ 9 ✢

JOE NOTICED WITH satisfaction that the emigrants' fires were becoming smaller now. As the train moved further and further away from available wood and they had to burn dry brush and twists of grass, the fires became smaller and smaller. The folks were learning.

In a few days, he calculated, they would reach the Platte. There would be wood there and water to refill the barrels. Joe just hoped they were learning well enough now to let them survive later in the journey. Out past the salt lake, there was some serious dry. The lessons needed to be well and truly learned before he took them into that.

As he passed through the wagons now, checking on the people and their gear, he tipped his hat to the ladies and murmured greetings to the gents and the children. It was a pleasant evening, the air fresh and cool without being chill. The moon was about two days from being full, and hung overhead like a huge lantern.

Over on the eastern fringe of the overnight camp, he saw

a brighter light showing beneath the belly of someone's wagon. A second glance showed this was not a fire but a collection of actual, normal-size lanterns. Joe altered course and ambled in that direction.

"Well, well, what d' we have here?" he asked as he came around the back of the rig. There were half a dozen men kneeling in a circle around a folded blanket. Each man had a tin cup and a small pile of coins in front of him. Sitting on the lazyboard extending from the side of the wagon was a keg. Joe frowned. He was fairly sure that keg was one he had seen before. Except that time it was strapped onto the back of one of Tharp's mules. Someone in the train must have bought one or maybe more of those kegs before Tharp's helpers turned back. If, that is, they really had turned back. He'd thought they were cowed enough to give up and go back to civilization. But then he'd been wrong in the past a time or two.

Still, it was no business of his if the men in this train wanted to take a drink. He was hired to be their guide, not their keeper.

"Evenin', Moss."

"Good evening, Charlie." He nodded. "Able. Jonas. McCarthy."

Brendan McCarthy seemed to be the one doing most of the winning, or so it looked by the size of the pile of coins in front of him. McCarthy gave Joe a look that was pure hate, but the man did not say anything. Fair enough, Joe figured. After what happened back in Missouri, it was only natural for him to feel that way.

"Enjoy your evening, gents," he said, and wandered on without commenting on their keg.

He heard a low buzz of whispers as he walked on, but made no attempt to hear what was being said. He was not being paid to be likable, and did not particularly care what

McCarthy and his cronies thought. Did not really care what they did either so long as they did not get out of line.

He had gone perhaps another fifty yards when he heard light footsteps approaching him from behind. Running, but so quietly as to barely be heard. If it was one of those men, McCarthy perhaps . . .

Joe waited until the person was close, then stopped and whirled, ready to meet an attack if that was what this was.

Instead, the moonlight revealed Fiona McCarthy's slim form. Joe snatched his hand away from the haft of his tomahawk hoping she had not seen him reach for it. He tipped his hat to her and said, "Good evening, miss. Something I can do for you?"

The girl stopped and bent at the waist. He assumed she was taking deep breaths. After a moment, she straightened and he could see her better. She was not wearing a bonnet this evening and her hair was hanging loose, falling almost to her waist. She must have been brushing it when she slipped out of the wagon to come after Joe. He wished the moon, bright though it was, was even brighter so he could see Fiona the better. She fair took his breath away, and he hadn't been running. It was just that she was that beautiful.

"Are you all right, miss?" he asked when she stood mute in the moonlight rather than answer his first inquiry. "Can I help you?"

After a moment Fiona nodded, but still she said nothing. Finally, she spoke. "I just wanted to . . . uh . . ."

"Yes?"

There was not light enough to see by, but he got the impression that Fiona very likely was blushing.

"I . . . well . . . I just wanted to thank you."

"You do? What for?"

"For, well, for not getting angry with Papa."

"You already thanked me for that days ago," Joe said.

"I meant, well, tonight."

"Why would I have gotten mad at him tonight?" he asked. He hadn't seen any reason for anger back there.

"For the, you know, the whiskey. You did see it, didn't you?"

"Oh, I saw it all right, but nobody was getting rowdy. Including your papa."

"He has mended his ways, Mr. Moss. He really has. And the whiskey . . . he says it is an investment. He intends to sell it along the way. To the other gentlemen a little at a time."

Joe thought about what the girl said, then grunted. "I don't know enough about cards and dice to know if your papa cheats, miss, but I hope he don't. 'Cause if he does, and if I find out about it, he is gonna be one awful unhappy soul to find himself out alone on the prairie with no wagon an' no wife to help him. But that isn't what you came out here t' hear, I know. I'm sorry to've said anything. You came out here t' say something nice and I've gone and turned things serious. Please forget I said anything. Will you do that for me?"

"Yes. Yes, I will." Her hand went to her throat and he thought she intended to say more, but she did not. After a moment, Fiona shook her head, then spun around in a swirl of flying skirts and ran back to her family's wagon.

God, that was one awfully pretty girl, he thought.

Not that he had any business thinking about her, Joe quickly amended. A girl like Fiona McCarthy deserved a fine gentleman. A *settled* gentleman. And one near to her own age. Why, Joe was 'most old enough to be her father. And Lord knows, he was anything but settled.

No, he was a fine choice for a dalliance but not for serious. Not for a decent girl like Fiona. Somebody like him, a wanderer, a brawler, a womanizer, and worse. No, the nicest thing he could do for Fiona McCarthy would be to stay far away from her.

But, oh, wasn't she the pretty one.

Joe stood watching until she was out of sight, then finally turned and continued making his evening rounds of the wagons.

JOE SWUNG INTO the saddle and laid his rifle across the pommel. He tugged his hat down and rose in the stirrups to take a look around. The wagons all seemed to be ready. Kramer and his boy stood beside their oxen ready for Joe to give the signal to lead out. He was about to do so when a woman came running into view from behind one of the rigs.

"Mr. Moss. Mr. Moss. You have to come, Mr. Moss."

"What's wrong, Mrs. Baxter?"

She slowed as she came closer and he could see that she was crying. "It is the Adams baby, Mr. Moss."

"The little one?" Joe couldn't help but smile whenever he saw the toddler. Tim and Agatha Adams's youngest was a cherub. Two years old or thereabouts and always smiling. Joe was positive he had never encountered a happier child anywhere.

"He is dead, Mr. Moss. He slipped away just now."

Joe felt a flush of sorrow. The boy was—had been—one

of three Adams children. They were good people, solid and sensible, and devoted to one another.

"I'll come see," he said, reining the paint around. He glanced at Samuel Kramer and shook his head. The train would not be rolling out today until they'd taken time to bury little . . . Joe thought the boy's name was Louis, but he was not positive about that. He'd always just called the child Button, as he did about half the kids in the bunch.

Joe followed Mrs. Baxter into the scattered tangle of wagons standing ready to leave. The Adams outfit was yoked up, but the tailgate of their wagon was down now and the canvas pulled open and he could not see any of the family. He rode around to the back of their rig and removed his hat as he leaned down to look inside.

Mrs. Adams, usually as bright and cheery as her baby, was seated atop a trunk holding the child to her breast and rocking back and forth while tears streamed down her face. Her husband and two other sons were huddled around her. Joe motioned for Tim to come out. He did so, but the boys stayed with their mother.

"I'm sorry, Tim. What happened?"

"He came down with a fever yesterday, Joe, or maybe it was the day before. Aggie didn't . . . we didn't either one of us think it was serious. Kids get sick easy but they get better just as easy. But this . . . last night he was burning up. Aggie sat up with him through the night and this morning he was quiet. We thought he was just resting. We thought he was getting better. You know?"

Joe nodded.

"He was . . . I went ahead and got my oxen hooked up ready to move. When I stuck my head inside to tell Aggie, she was crying. She said . . . she said Louie shuddered and turned blue and just . . . died. He died, Joe. I can't believe it.

I know kids die sometimes. Everybody knows that. But . . . we've never lost one of ours before. I wish . . ." Adams did not complete the sentence; the expression on his face displayed his anguish better than words could have anyway.

"I'll pass the word, Tim, but we won't hold up too awful long. I'm sorry, but we'll want to bury the little fellow here. We'll put a marker over him, of course." Whatever sort of cairn or marker they placed would be gone by the end of this season, the grave lost to everything except memory, but Joe did not intend to tell that to Tim or Agatha.

"Can't we possibly . . ."

"No, Tim. I'm sorry."

Mrs. Baxter went clucking into the Adams wagon, then soon emerged again and started making the rounds of the other wagons, spreading the news and summoning the other womenfolk to help Agatha prepare the child's body. They would wash and dress him and sew little Louis into his favorite blanket, perhaps with a cherished toy to keep him company. It was a ritual Joe had seen all too often before, and was the most difficult to bear when it was a child's life that had been cut short.

"Where's your shovel, Tim? We'd best prepare a place for him. Let me tell the others, then I'll come back and help you. But, Tim. Your other boys. Are they sick too?"

"No, they're fine. I'm sure of it."

Joe nodded and reined away. He hoped Tim was right about that. He'd seen what sickness could do to a train of emigrants if an epizootic ran ragged inside such a small and isolated community as a wagon train on the prairie. That was not something he hoped to see again. Just for the sake of caution, though, he thought it would be best if he asked a few questions of the other families while he was telling them about the Adamses' loss.

* * *

Joe waited until Samuel Kramer finished reading over the little boy's body, then pulled Kramer aside while Tim and some of the other men got busy filling the tiny grave and piling stones over top of it to keep coyotes and other carrion-eaters away.

"I need for you to call the company officers together, Samuel."

"Is something wrong, Joe?"

"Something is very wrong, I'm afraid. There are at least five more cases of fever in the train right now. If this keeps up, we may have more graves to dig."

"Oh, God! What can we do?"

"The first thing, Samuel, we need to find out if there are any more cases that I don't know about. Folks have to be warned, have to be told what to do when someone does come down with a fever. Anyone who is sick should be given plenty of water to drink. That's my experience. Water seems to help, though I sure don't know why."

"But we don't have much water. You know that as well as I do. Between what we use and the livestock and how long it has been since we left the last stream . . ."

"I know, but we have no choice if you want to keep the dying down. Those of us who aren't sick will just have to do without for a while. What water we have will go first to the sick and then to the animals. The rest of us will have to make do as best we can."

"But . . ."

"Which brings me to the next thing we need to do. We need to get to the Platte as quick as we can. We need water, lots of it, and we need wood. I'll explain why later, but it's important that we reach the river soon if we're to keep this from getting out of hand. As soon as the burying is done, Samuel, we're going to cut straight for the Platte and we aren't going to stop until we get there. We'll push the oxen hard. They can rest when we get to the river. So can the people. I calculate we can get there tomorrow, mid-morning maybe, if we keep on through the night. Normally, I'd say we are two and a half days from the river. I think we can cut that time considerable if we push ourselves hard enough. We won't stop to sleep nor to cook. I'll call breaks now and then just long enough to water the stock, but that is the only reason we'll slow down."

"But, Joe, we can't do that. We have women, kids, now sick folks too. Why, to keep walking all night long without food or rest, it simply would be too much."

"Will it be any easier, Samuel, if we have dead to bury instead of sick to tend?"

Kramer sighed. "Are you sure, Joe?"

"Unfortunately, Samuel, yes. I am."

The emigrant company's president sighed again and nodded. "I'll get the officers together. We will impress on everyone that we have to do this."

"Good man, Samuel."

✛ 11 ✛

B Y THE TIME the wagons reached the south bank of the Platte, there were seven more cases of fever in the train. Seven more that they knew about. Joe realized there probably were even more in such early stages that they were not apparent, possibly not even to those who were sick.

Judging from some of the grim expressions he saw around him, Joe suspected some of the emigrants were close to panic. That became only worse when a woman named Duchins fell down in a faint after finding her ailing husband dead in the back of their wagon.

Joe hurriedly called the people together. They crowded close together, anxious and afraid. Joe let down the tailgate of the nearest wagon—he did not even look to see whose it was—and stepped up onto it so he could see out over the crowd. And so he could be seen by them.

A good many of the women, he noticed, were crying. Those who had small children tended to keep them clutched tight against their skirts, like broody hens holding their chicks under wing.

"We have to split apart. We're catching this from each other, dammit. We have to get away from it," someone shouted. But if the train broke apart now, many of the people would very likely contract the fevers and die in isolation, unable to help each other pull through.

"Now hold on there," Joe responded in a commanding voice, raising his arms and calling attention back to himself. "That is *not* the way. I've seen these epizootics before. I know what we have to do."

"Then for God's sakes, Mr. Moss, tell us," a woman's voice called.

"Sweat lodges," Joe returned. "We have to build sweat lodges. We have to break the fevers. Once the fever is broken, we have to give them water, lots of water, all they can stomach. If we do that, there isn't a person here who can't fight this thing off."

That was not entirely true, and he knew it. The very old, the very young, and those who were already infirm were especially vulnerable and might not survive. This did not seem like the proper moment to get into that unhappy likelihood, however. A man without hope can die of a hangnail, or so it sometimes seemed to him, while someone with grit and determination will surmount impossible odds. When he first came to the mountains as a trapper, young and ignorant, Joe once met a man who had been attacked by a grizzly bear. The beast ripped one of the man's arms off with a single swipe of its paw, then took his head in its mouth. The plucky fellow killed the bear with his knife, then found thorns to pin his scalp together—the skin kept sliding down over what was left of his face so that he could not see— and holed up for a few days to begin healing. He used the dead bear for food until the meat began to go putrid, then walked out to rejoin his band of trappers. When Joe met him five or six years later, the fellow was still in the mountains, although he had given up trapping for himself and gone to trading with the Indians for his livelihood.

"What's a sweat lodge?" Thomas Harvey asked. Harvey had four daughters and Joe knew that one of them had already come down sick.

"It's an Indian remedy," Joe explained, "and it works mighty well. We will build as many as we need. Put up a framework of saplings and drape a canvas wagon cover over top of it to hold the heat. We'll need fires. Big fires. To heat rocks. You heat the rocks in the fires and then put the rocks inside the lodges. Throw dippers of water on the hot rocks to make steam. The wet heat eases the lungs and lets a person breathe the better an' it helps to break the fever too.

"Now I want every man and boy busy. You, Jim, and you, you, and you over there, I want you t' cut young tree growth for the frames. You, you, and you can start building the frames. The rest o' you men and the bigger boys gather wood for the fires. And rocks. Does anybody have anything we can use as a sledge to drag the stone?"

"I don't have a sledge but we can use my trailer. I'll empty it out and we can use that."

"How about tailgates? Lord knows, we got enough oxen to pull. We can just chain to a tailgate and use that for a sledge."

"That's a good idea," Joe said, encouraging their ingenuity to get the job done. "We need plenty of firewood, mind you, and plenty of stone. Choose rocks big enough to hold the heat but small enough we can pick them up and move them easy." He smiled. "Don't forget, we have to move them from the fire to the inside of the lodge while they're hot, so you won't want to rassle with them. Find stones about this big or thereabouts." With his hands he indicated an object the size of a gallon basket more or less.

"And don't forget blankets," he added. "When a person's fever has broke an' they're being brought out of the sweat lodge, you don't want to let them catch a chill or they'll not only go sick again, they'll be worse off than they were to start with. When they come out, you'll want to bundle them up in blankets. Keep them warm and keep on giving them water. Lots and lots of water. I can't tell you why that helps for the truth is that I don't know. But I do know that it does help. I reckon that's what counts.

"Ladies, while the men are building the lodges and getting everything together, I want you to check on how many people we got in this train who are sick, already sick, or coming down sick. Pay special mind to the children. Now let's all get busy. We're all of us gonna pitch in together and we are gonna beat this thing."

The assembly broke apart as people hurried to tend to their own, to check on their friends, and to begin the tasks Joe had set for them. Joe hopped down from the back of the wagon he'd been using—the wagon belonged to Vance Clayborne, he noticed now—and motioned for Sam Kramer to join him. Drawing Kramer off to the side, he added, "Something else, Samuel. We need to get a burial detail together. We'll be needing graves."

"But I thought you said you can cure the sick," Kramer said.

"I hope everybody does survive. But I don't truly expect it. Besides, there's already Mr. Duchins."

"Oh, yes. Jim. God help me, I forgot about him lying dead over there."

"And we need to get him in the ground right quick. That's something else I've noticed that can help. The Indians, someone of them dies like that, what they'll do is fire the man's lodge and burn him and everything in his tipi. Then the rest of 'em pack up and move along. They say it's to get away from the spirits that caused the death. Now I don't pretend to know nothing about spirits and all that. But getting far away from the dead seems to help."

"And these sweat lodges you spoke of? Do they genuinely help too?"

"They sure do, Samuel. They're what is gonna let us beat this thing."

"But we still will need graves?"

Joe nodded. "I'm afraid so. Some anyhow. But we don't want t' make a show of that. Better to keep it quiet. Do it, of course. But quiet, if you see what I mean."

"Yes. All right. I, uh, I will see to it."

Joe turned away and went to begin supervising the laying out of several sweat lodges, each of which would be big enough to accommodate several victims of the fever. They would separate the men from the women, of course, but put several folks together in the lodges for the sake of efficiency.

"Not too tall," Joe advised his construction workers. "We want to fill them up with steam, so let's not make that any harder than it has to be. And put them close to the water. Along here, I think. We'll put the fire in the middle of the lodges so we won't lose much in the way of heat when we move the stones between the fire and the lodge. Lodges here and here, I think, and over there. Yes, the fire here. And we can pile the stones right here."

"Are you sure this is the right thing for us to be doing, Mr. Moss? My Emma . . . I think she's getting feverish."

"I am positive, Ted. Now let's get busy and do it, what d'you say."

The man nodded agreement, but his expression was full of uncertainty.

"Stay the course, Ted," Joe advised gently. "Have faith."

"But in a remedy used by savages?"

"Yes. Because it works."

The man sighed. Then reached for a bundle of saplings one of the others brought at a run.

✛ 12 ✛

JOE'S EYES BURNED and stung. Lack of sleep. Heat and ash from the huge, roaring fire. Sweat from those moments when he was inside one of the huts to carry in fresh stones or fling dippers of water onto the heated rocks. All of that, and he still did not know if they were going to prevail over this devastating fever.

Already, they'd lost the Adams boy and Duchins and now Theo Mabry's mother-in-law. Joe felt like they were swimming upstream. And the current was awfully strong.

Still, a man does what he can. Everything he can. After that . . . after that he accepts whatever comes.

"Don't try an' carry that rock, Pete," Joe advised a half-grown boy whose father had the fever. "You'll break your back trying to carry it. Maybe break the shovel too. Just prod the rock onto the blade o' your shovel and drag it. Kind of sled or skid it. Yeah, that's right. That's better. Go on now. You want to get it there while it's still hot."

He took his hat off and wiped the sweat out of his eyes,

then glanced toward the west. It would be dark again soon. They'd labored all yesterday afternoon and through the night and now for nearly another day. The truth was that Joe was becoming discouraged.

His spirits lifted some when he saw Fiona McCarthy's approach. Her face was streaked with sweat that made tracks through the soot from the fire, and still she was just about the prettiest thing he'd ever in his life seen. She looked worried, though.

"Are you all right, Miss McCarthy?"

"No, I . . . my mama. She has the fever. She's come down with it too."

"There's room in that lodge over there. Get her settled. I'll come see if there's anything I can do."

"No, I . . . my papa says this isn't doing any good. He says no good can come from it, that sweating just weakens a body and makes them worse. He says he won't allow Mama to be abused like this. He says . . . he says he will not allow her to be put in one of those places with all the sick people. He says she will just get worse from breathing the air in there."

A retort rose to Joe's lips, but got no further than that. The fact was that Fiona's father was an asshole, pure and simple. Probably, he objected to the treatment largely because it was Joe who proposed it; therefore, it had to be bad, at least in Brendan's mind.

"Would he allow her to be put into a lodge by herself then if he doesn't want her exposed to others who have the fever?" Joe asked.

"I don't know. He might."

"Go back to your wagon, Fiona. Convince him to allow her to breathe the steam. She needs it. I'll build another lodge. A small one just for her. Go on now, please. I'll build the frame, then come fetch the wagon cover off your rig."

"I can't ask you to—"

"You didn't ask. I offered. Go now. If she has the fever, there's no sense wasting time."

Fiona nodded and hurried away. Joe got some of the left-over saplings and a shovel so he could start on the framework, lashing the limber poles together with twists of bark. That would last long enough for the work that needed to be done here.

He chose a spot a few paces apart from the larger community lodges and made a low shelter, then hurried to the McCarthy wagon. Fiona's mother was lying atop a platform of crates in the bed of the wagon. The woman was fully dressed, but was not covered by blankets.

"She'll catch a chill like that, girl. Don't you have something to cover her with?"

"She says she's too hot. Burning up. Papa says she needs a chance to cool off."

"What she needs is to sweat that fever out. Cover her. I'll get the canvas off your wagon if you don't mind."

Joe hadn't seen Brendan at first. Now he did. The man was hollow-eyed and gaunt, and for a moment Joe thought the father had fever too. Or possibly was drunk. That opinion changed when Joe got closer. The man, he saw, was frightened. Joe could see the fear and the worry in his eyes.

The man was an asshole and a son of a bitch, no question about it. But he also seemed to care very much about his wife. He was wrong about the sweat treatment, damn him. But he was sincere. Joe did not doubt that. Not after seeing him like this.

McCarthy looked at Joe with mute anguish and offered no objection when Joe worked his way quickly around the wagon to untie the canvas cover and pull it free.

He took the wagon cover back toward the riverbank and draped it in place over the frame he'd built and weighted the edges with rocks, then hurried back to the McCarthy wagon. He was pleased to see that Mrs. McCarthy was wrapped in a quilt this time.

"Here we go," he said, sliding the woman's limp form closer and lifting her over the end gate. Joe cradled her in his arms and carried her to the waist-high hut, Fiona following close beside them.

"You'll need to help me now, girl. Get inside and help me get her comfortable in there. Then I'll go bring some hot stones and water to start making steam."

"All right." Fiona helped get her mother settled; then Joe hurried away to bring hot stones and a pail of water.

By the time they were done with that, night had fallen, the camp illuminated now by the tall flame from the fire where they continued to heat rocks for the several sweat lodges.

It looked like a scene from Hell, Joe thought. The question was whether it was doing any good.

The fire blazed high for three days and nights more. By the end of that time, the men of the train were having to forage for wood a mile and a half up and down the river. People were exhausted. Nerves were on edge. But they had not lost another soul to the fever, and most of those who had come down with it were on the mend now, outside the sweat lodges wrapped chin-high in blankets and taking in all the fluids they could hold. They were shaky and weak, but no longer in danger. In the past twenty-four hours, only one new case had been discovered. Fiona McCarthy now lay beside her mother in the small hut Joe had built for her.

Joe knelt at the foot of the lodge and tugged a fold of

canvas aside so he could stick his head and shoulders in. He scattered a dipper full of water onto the stones that lay between the two women and took a look at both. The last time he had been here, delivering freshly heated stones, Mrs. McCarthy had been delirious, thrashing back and forth and rambling incoherently. Now her eyes were open and she seemed fully aware of her surroundings. Fiona looked like she was sleeping. Or unconscious.

He wanted to feel of Fiona's forehead to gauge the severity of her fever, but did not want to jostle either of them. One of the effects of the fever was acute pain in the joints and muscles. For most of its victims, any slight touch could be like driving spikes into their flesh. He certainly did not want to cause either woman to suffer that, so he withdrew from the lodge and laid the cover carefully back in place, then walked around to the head of the lodge so he could open that end and check on their temperatures.

"Fiona, dear? Fiona? Are you awake, Fiona?"

"Yes, Mama. What do you want?" She sounded groggy and half asleep.

Joe was kneeling close to their heads, and could hear them through the canvas as if he were included in the conversation. It was not his intention to eavesdrop, but he still wanted to feel their temperatures, so he remained where he was for the moment.

"Where is your daddy, sweetheart?"

"I don't know, Mama."

Joe knew. Brendan McCarthy seemed to have the constitution of one of his oxen. With half the train down sick and some of its members already dead, Brendan McCarthy was fit as a fiddle . . . and drunk as a lord. The man had been drinking since they stopped to treat the fevers, drinking up the whiskey he had intended to sell along the way. The last time Joe saw him, McCarthy was passed out in the back of his wagon. Joe had tried to rouse him so he could take his oxen to water, but McCarthy was too far gone for that. Joe despised the son of a bitch but rather than see the animals suffer, he led them to the river and tended them himself. He expected Brendan was still there. Or no further away from that spot than the nearest whiskey keg.

"I wish . . . I wish I could see him one more time." Mrs. McCarthy's voice came softly through the canvas. She sounded weak.

"You will, Mama. Papa will be here soon."

Wishful thinking, Joe thought. But harmless enough.

"No, I . . . I am going soon, sweet child."

"Don't talk like that, Mama. It scares me."

"I can feel it, dear. I'll be gone before the day is done. Will you mark my grave, Fiona? Please tell me you will."

"Mama, you aren't going to—"

"Just promise me." There was a small sound that might have been a laugh. "Someday. Even if it isn't right away. Will you do that for me? Please?"

"All right, Mama. Someday. When you . . . when it happens. Someday a long time from now."

"Thank you, dear. Promise me something else, Fiona."

"Mama!"

"This . . . this is important, dear. I want you to promise me"—she coughed and spit—"want you to promise . . . Fiona, my lovely child, you know . . . you know your daddy is not . . . he is not strong, dear. He is gruff and angry sometimes, but he is not strong. Not like you and me. We are strong. Your daddy . . . when I am gone, dear, he will need you. He doesn't know how much he will need you to take care of him. Fiona, I want you to promise that you will take care of your daddy . . . when I am gone . . . take care . . . of him. Stay with him. Promise."

"Mama, I . . ."

"Promise, Fiona. Take care of your daddy always. He will need you ever so much."

There was another rather muffled sound. A sob perhaps. Joe was not sure.

"Mama, you aren't going to die."

"Then it will do no harm for you to make the promise, will it."

"All right, Mama."

"Say it. I want to hear you say it."

"Mama, I promise you, I will take care of papa if . . . if something happens to you . . . someday."

"You mustn't break a promise made to a dying person, Fiona. A dying promise is solemn. Never forget it. Never."

"You are not going to die, Mama."

"I am not afraid of dying, Fiona, my precious. I want you to know that. I am not afraid at all. Isn't that wonderful, dear? Isn't that a blessing? Fiona, when you bury me, please put your Grandmother Cutchall's old Bible with me. But I want you to have her locket. You remember the one. It is in the steel box."

"Mama, please stop talking like this. You aren't going to die. I . . . I won't let you."

"Oh, but I want to talk, dear. I will not have any more chances, and there is so much I want to say to you."

Mrs. McCarthy's voice was growing weaker, but her spirit seemed strong enough. And her determination to continue talking.

Joe had wanted to check on their fevers, but he really did not want to intrude on such private conversation. He could check them the next time he refreshed the hot stones in their hut, he decided.

Very carefully, so as to make no sound, he crept back from the head of the lodge and silently left to see to others of the sick.

When Joe returned to the little hut an hour or so later, he found Fiona weeping bitterly and her mother lying dead beside her.

✢ 13 ✢

SOME OF THE other men in the train tried to get Brendan McCarthy sober enough to see to his wife's burial, but the best they could do was to prop him upright beside the grave. Joe was not at all sure that Brendan knew what was going on.

They put Margaret McCarthy in the ground without much in the way of ceremony, although Samuel Kramer read a few words over her, as he had done for the others who died. Fiona was not there, and did not even know that her mother was being buried. Joe hadn't told her. He was sure if she knew, she would attend, would crawl if she had to, and if there was anything a person in her condition did not need, it was to become chilled now.

And he was sure that asshole father of hers hadn't told her. Brendan was not able to walk that far. He did, however, manage to keep himself supplied with whiskey from one of his kegs.

When the burying was done with, Joe dipped a cup of

broth out of one of the communal pots that was kept hot beside the fire. They did not have birds to spare so they could make chicken soup for the ailing, but he was able to shoot enough prairie chickens to make do. He did not know if the broth actually did any good, but providing it gave the women something constructive to do, and that was a benefit right there. People who are busy, he'd noticed in the past, don't seem to get sick as often or as seriously as those who are idle.

He carried the broth to the lodge where Fiona lay, and crawled in beside her.

The girl was burning up with fever. He touched the back of his hand to her brow, and was startled by how hot she was. Dangerously hot, dammit, but he did not know anything more to do for her.

He sat cross-legged beside her and very gently lifted her head.

"Fiona. Wake up, girl. I have something for you."

Her eyelids fluttered, but she remained asleep. Or unconscious. Joe was afraid she was falling into a coma. One she might never come out of.

He set the tin cup of broth aside and pulled Fiona into his arms, cradling her like an infant. Since she'd come down with the fever, it seemed like she was shrinking, diminishing in size as her spirit withered away. When he held her, she was little more than bone covered with skin and a few scraps of meat.

Her cheeks were hollow and there were dark half-moons under her eyes. Her neck seemed too slender to support a wisp of hair, much less her head.

Yet even so, she was the most beautiful thing Joe Moss ever saw.

And even in this condition, with Fiona emaciated and burning up with fever, he felt a stirring of desire when he held her. There was something about this girl that moved him as no other had ever done. Even now he wanted her. He was grateful she was unconscious. Otherwise, she would surely feel his response to the touch of her body against his. She would be scandalized. Worse, if she ever suspected, Joe was sure she would avoid him forevermore.

If she lived. If she lived.

Joe touched her cheek. Shook her head back and forth just a little in an attempt to wake her. "Fiona. Open your eyes, girl. You got to wake up. Just a little. Come back, Fiona. Come back here from wherever you've gone to."

He held her tight against his chest and stroked her hair, smoothing it back from her face. Her hair was dry and lifeless.

"Wake up, Fiona. You got to wake up, girl."

Fiona's breath caught. Stopped completely for a moment before it resumed. Her eyelids fluttered, and there was a matching butterfly sensation deep in Joe's belly. He had faced armed men in duels to the death, but he was sure he never before had been this frightened. He thought sure the girl was dying there in his arms.

"Fiona, girl. Come back. Please." He hugged her and continued to stroke and gentle her. After a moment, her ragged breathing steadied.

"Wake up, Fiona. Please." The rough hand that had been smoothing her hair moved over her face as if he were trying to memorize the feel of her features. He touched her cheeks. Her throat. Her nose and lips.

Fiona gasped and her mouth gaped open as she sucked in breath. He felt her shudder and then grow still. Joe was sure she was going, but after a few moments more she resumed breathing normally.

"Fiona," he whispered. "Look at me. Open your eyes an' look at me."

Incredibly, marvelously, she did. Her eyelids fluttered again and she opened her eyes. He felt fairly sure she did not recognize him or her surroundings. She seemed oblivious to the world around her. She had sunk into some misty world within. But she was responsive. A little.

Joe fumbled on the ground beside him for the cup of broth and held it to her dry, cracked lips. He tipped a little of the thin broth into her mouth. Half of it ran back out again. But half remained, and he saw her throat move as she involuntarily swallowed the liquid that was in her mouth.

"Good. That's good. Now a little more."

He trickled more broth into her. Patiently wiped away whatever ran back out. And poured again. And again. And yet again until Fiona lashed her head back and forth in rejection of the bland soup. Her forehead banged Joe painfully on the mouth hard enough to draw blood. He did not mind that in the least. She had taken some of the broth. That would give her strength to fight this fever. Strength enough?

Joe held Fiona McCarthy until his arms went numb and his back ached, but he did not place her back onto her bed until she was sleeping and breathing easy. And he would not have let go of her then except he needed to bring more hot stones and more water to create the steam she needed to keep her lungs open.

Joe Moss was not a praying man. Not in the ordinary sense. But he found himself now silently offering up a Cheyenne chant to whatever spirits there were who might hear and help.

He tucked the blankets tight around Fiona, swaddling her up to her chin; then he crawled out of the sweat lodge and hurried to fetch hot stones and water.

He wanted . . . he would not let this girl die, damn it. He would not!

* * *

Joe felt Fiona stiffen. He was holding her again, rocking her gently to and fro. She had been sleeping fitfully for the past hour since he returned to the lodge and took her into his arms. He was becoming increasingly worried about her. This was . . . he had to take a moment to think back; his thoughts were muddled from lack of sleep . . . this was the fourth day she had been virtually in a coma and he did not know what else to do for her.

Her forehead was dry and her skin brittle. She needed fluids. He knew that, but he could not get her to accept anything. He poured soup into her. Water. Rose-hip tea. Chamomile. Everything he could pick, find, or borrow. He would part her lips and tip the liquids into her. Moments later, it would all run back out again. All Joe could do was to patiently clean her chin and throat to mop up the spill and then try again. He did not think any of it was reaching her stomach. But he could not stop trying.

He chanted—aloud now much of the time and the hell with what the emigrants might think about that—and he prayed to the Christian god as well, even though he knew almost nothing about the faith that sustained Samuel Kramer and so many of the others in the train. At one point on his trips out of Fiona's lodge to fetch fresh stones and more water, he found Kramer surrounded by a group of the menfolk and enlisted the company president's support.

"Pray for her, Samuel. I don't know about praying. Don't know a damn thing about it. But that's a trail you seem t' know. I'd appreciate it if you'd lead the way on that one."

Joe asked Samuel Kramer to help, but he carefully, deliberately avoided any contact with Brendan McCarthy. Joe figured that useless son of a bitch would stay drunk until he ran out of liquor again. After that . . .

After that nothing. Joe could not have it out with

McCarthy. Never would be able to. His feelings for Fiona were much too strong to permit it. How could he ever look the girl in the eye again if he killed her father? Joe might as well kill himself as McCarthy. It would be kinder to Fiona to do it that way. But, oh, he despised the drunken bastard. No good to his wife; no good to his daughter; no good to anyone that Joe could see. And there was nothing, absolutely nothing, that Joe could do about it except to avoid him.

He felt Fiona stiffen now and tremble. Her eyes flew open and she tried to speak.

She was staring fearfully toward the canvas roof of the little lodge where she lay so grievously ill. She seemed to be looking at something there although there was nothing Joe lifted his eyes in the direction Fiona was peering to make sure of it—nothing there for her to see.

She tried to speak but no sound came out, only a puff of breath rank with illness and tinged with the stink of death.

Joe smelled the fever that was eating her from within. She was within hours, perhaps minutes, of dying.

He knew that and he could do nothing more to help her.

He clutched her close to his breast and covered her dear face with light butterfly kisses.

And washed her cheeks with his tears.

Fiona was leaving him, and Joe Moss did not know how to accept the loss. He'd found her so late. Too late.

All he could do was hold her very close and continue to rock back and forth.

And to pray. Untutored. Uncertain. But sincere. God knows he was sincere in his awkward attempts to fetch Fiona McCarthy back from the precipice.

"FEELING BETTER?"

Fiona nodded. "A lot better now, thanks." She leaned very lightly on Joe's arm as she walked beside the river. It was her first outing since the fever broke and she began to mend. That was two days earlier. This morning, she had been able to hold down the broth that over the past few days she had come to loathe, and half of one of Mrs. Hallett's biscuits. Joe figured if she ate one of *his* biscuits, she would be back in a sickbed immediately after.

Here, now, walking beside Fiona, Joe Moss was conscious of nature's beauty. The glorious colors of the sunrise painting wisps of cloud with pink and gold and a thousand colors that Joe had no names for. The feel of the air and the freshness of its scent. The sight of grass rippling in the breeze. The sight of oxen grazing. And yes, the sights and sounds of the emigrants going about their morning tasks. Somehow, Fiona's presence opened Joe's eyes to the beauty of the most mundane things and made him value and appreciate them.

"What are you thinking?" Her voice brought him back from reverie.

"I . . . nothing. Really."

She stopped and looked at him closely. Then she smiled. "Why, Joseph, you are blushing. What *were* you thinking?" She laughed, as if satisfied that she had her answer.

"I am not," he insisted.

Fiona only laughed again. And leaned the more heavily on Joe's arm as they resumed their walk.

"I'd like to ask you something," she said a few moments later as she looked out across the Platte, slanting sunlight sparkling and dancing on its surface. "But you have to promise you won't think I am being foolish. Promise you won't laugh."

"All right, I reckon that's a promise I can make."

"While I was crazy with the fever. I thought . . . I thought I was floating. Or being carried. And . . . you were there. I could see your face. I could feel . . . it was like you touched my face. And you were singing. Ever so soft and gentle. Did . . . did you do that? Was I imagining things, Joseph, or was that real?"

He had held her. Kissed her. Whispered chants for her. He had done all those things. Now he blushed again.

Fiona stopped and reached up. She touched his cheek, then ran her fingertips lightly over Joe's eyes and onto his lips. The scent of her was strong. He wanted to take this girl into his arms and . . . He moved slightly apart from her. People were watching. Fiona's reputation would be ruined if anyone saw and thought the worst. And if anyone saw, they were very likely to think the worst. Hell, they were very likely to be right in what they thought too, at least as far as Joe's intentions were concerned.

"You don't have to answer that either," Fiona said. "I

know." She moved closer again and pressed her cheek against his chest. "Thank you, Joseph."

Then she pulled away from him and smiled. "I am ever so much better now. Thank you." The spell, whatever it was that had been between them for that moment, was gone. But it was a moment that Joe would remember. A moment he would cherish.

"Why do you call me Joseph now?" he asked, trying to return to normalcy. "Everyone else in the train calls me Joe. I haven't been called Joseph since . . . in a very long time."

"Could we stop here? I'm getting a little tired."

"I'm sorry. I should have thought, you bein' down so sick for s' long. It wouldn't be good for you t' do too much now. Here. Sit on this tuft of sweet grass." He sat cross-legged beside her. Not too close, though.

"I don't know why," she said, and at first Joe could not remember what the question had been. "Joseph just seems to fit you. Do you mind?"

He shook his head. "No. I don't mind."

Fiona smiled and Joe felt . . . he did not dare admit to what he felt even though he could not deny it. And would not willingly relinquish it either. "Why, Joseph. Are you blushing yet again?"

Joe ducked his head and turned his face away. Fiona laughed. She sounded pleased. That was good. That was worth anything. Giving her pleasure was worth everything.

Joe cleared his throat and reached into his possibles bag for his pipe and twist of tobacco. He needed something to keep his hands busy and his mind occupied.

He heard Fiona chuckle. She did not seem to mind in the least.

"Folks. Everybody. Quiet down now an' listen to me," Joe said loudly. He was standing on the tailgate of Simon

Taylor's wagon. The people were gathered near. Behind them were the skeletal frames of the sweat lodges. The huts were abandoned now, the canvas covers returned to the wagons where they belonged.

"We've been stopped here the better part o' two weeks. That is time lost that we can't get back. We need t' get moving again if we want to get across the mountains while the passes are still open. Get yourselves and your gear in order tonight, for tomorrow morning we'll pull out an' get on the road again. Tonight, though, we're gonna take a little time to remember the folks that we lost here." He turned and pointed.

"We've left eight graves over there, and Sam wants to hold, like, a little prayer service to remember them. For my part of things, I just want t' remind you to see to your rigs. Make sure your axles are greased and your spokes are tight. We pull out first light t'morra. Samuel . . ."

Joe hopped down from the wagon and let Kramer step up to take his place and lead the memorial service. He could see Fiona and her father over to the left. Brendan looked to be sober. Son of a bitch must have run out of liquor, Joe thought.

Kramer began speaking, reading from the Book and talking about what he read.

Joe slipped quietly away from the gathering and went to tend to his own affairs. He was only mildly concerned about the time they'd lost here. It had been necessary regardless. And they had gotten an early enough start that he thought these days would not make much of a difference.

Besides, a man takes what comes and copes with it the best way he knows how. That is all he can do.

✠ 15 ✠

J OE COULDN'T FIGURE out what all the excitement was
about. The train had come to a complete halt. Women
were babbling and men were clutching their rifles and shotguns, those few who owned guns—although at least half
the emigrants did not. The young girls had disappeared completely, and the boys in the train were practically coming
out of their skins they were so eager, yet at the same time
skittish.

All of that, and the only thing in sight other than their
own wagon train was a little band of Indians, eighteen or
twenty of them on the move somewhere with their families
and three scrawny, bony, worn-down little ponies dragging
heavily loaded travois behind them. There was nothing
identifiable about them—they looked like a band of raga-
muffin beggars more than anything else—but he expected
they would likely be Ottoes or maybe Sacs, one of the unim-
portant tribes in any event. Certainly, they posed no threat
greater than transmitting lice if you got too close to them.

The thing was, these were very likely the first "wild" Indians these emigrants had ever seen. Hell, maybe they'd never even encountered the tamed variety back wherever it was all these people came from.

"Calm down, everyone. There's no need to get excited." He passed his message over and over again as he rode back and forth beside the wagons. He might just as well have ordered the clouds to halt their drift across the sky. "These people don't mean you no harm. Gerald, put that shotgun back in your wagon. You keep waving it around like that, you're gonna have an accident an' hurt somebody. Jones, dammit, you're letting your leader get acrost the chains. Straighten your team out, man, before you have a wreck. Leon, where d'you think you're going? Get back with your rig. We got better things t' do than stand around staring. Everybody, for Pete's sake calm down an' quit acting like we're about t' be attacked by pirates or something."

Joe shook his head. All the talking in the world would not do any good here. About all he could do was to stop the damn train for the day and let them get this out of their systems. Let them get used to the idea that there really were Indians out here. And that not every Indian wanted to kill them and take their scalps for souvenirs.

"All right. All right, dammit, circle up and break your hitches. We'll stay here tonight." It was barely past noon and they were losing hours of daylight, but under the circumstances, he supposed this was for the best.

Kramer came trotting over to where Joe was sitting on the gray horse he'd inherited—more or less—from that bastard Tharp. "Are we in danger? Should we prepare for an attack? Will we have to post guards?"

"You aren't in no danger from these people," Joe told him. "They're harmless enough. They won't start no fight or anything. But yes, you'll want t' put a couple men with the livestock tonight, an' pass the word around for everybody to watch out when the Indians are walking by. They're apt t' carry off anything they can get their hands on, so be careful t' not let them."

"Are you sure. . . ."

"I'm sure, Samuel. Now pass that word if you will. I'm gonna go have a word with them before they mix in with the train."

Joe gigged the gray and put it into a lope toward the band of Indians, who were still two hundred yards or so distant and moving east toward the wagon train. As he came near, he saw just how ragged these people were. There were only three males of useful age. The rest were women, runny-nose kids, and old folk. Two of the old-timers were so wrinkled and shriveled up that he could not decide if they were male or female. Not that it mattered.

He greeted them in two different languages, but received an answer that was confined to hand movements in the universal sign language of the plains. Joe grunted and responded in kind. A few minutes later, he spun the gray and returned to where a rather anxious-looking Samuel Kramer and some of the men were waiting.

"What is it, Joe? Are they hostile?"

"Lord, no," he told them. "They're a bunch of raggedy-ass Rees, blanket Indians from one of the forts back along the Missouri, that thought they'd leave the protection o' the soldiers an' go back to living fat and free out on the grass. Except things ain't like they used to be. This close to civilization, the buffalo are mostly used up or scattered to hell an' gone. There's not a gun amongst them, just some pissant bows an' throwing sticks. I think they been living off rabbits and prairie dogs mostly."

Joe swung around in his saddle. "Eddie, d'you still have some of that deer meat?"

"Yeah, but it's green as grass now, Joe. You know that. I been feeding it to my dog."

"Then do me a favor, please. Let me have it. I'll carry it to those Rees. It will make them happy as pigs in slop."

"Joe, that meat ain't fit for human folks. It's spoiled bad."

"It's good enough if a person is hungry enough. Which this bunch is. You notice there's no dogs with them? They've already eaten all o' those that they had. That spoiled deer meat will be a feast for them. They'll cut off the worst of it an' boil whatever is left. The bones alone will be enough to make them a good feed."

"You're welcome to it if you really think so."

"I do, and I thank you. The rest of you settle down now an' tell your families to leave the Indians be. If they come around, you might wanta give them a scrap of something to eat, but mind you don't get carried away with generosity you can't afford. You're gonna see an awful lot of hungry Indians along the way, and all you got for yourselves is what you're carrying with you. Before we get to the Californias, you might regret whatever you give away now. Keep that in mind."

Joe turned the gray away, then wheeled it back again. "I almost forgot. You grown men and your older boys might take a notion to get yourselves a piece of red meat tonight. Anybody wants to know what it's like to fuck a Indian, you'll have your chance. Cheap too. A couple pennies or some biscuits and you can pretty much take your pick. Not that there's a pretty one in the bunch. I've already looked. But you should ought to know that blanket Indians like these that've lived close around the forts, they're likely carrying the clap and crabs and who the hell knows what else. So if you do dip your wicks, you'd best go scrub your weapon mighty good just as quick as you're done." Joe grinned. "Personally, I'd recommend you dunk your peckers in boiling water just to be sure you get them clean again. But that's up t' you."

Kramer looked like he was genuinely shocked. But Joe noticed that some of the men, including several of the married ones, were more thoughtful than offended.

"You can't . . . surely you aren't serious about that, Mr. Moss," one of the men gasped. "B-*boil* it?"

Joe nodded, just as solemn as he could be. "I've done it myself many a time, Jim. It hurts, o' course, but not for long. No, sir, it don't take long at all to decide if it's been in there long enough." Joe chuckled softly as he turned the gray away once more. "Come along, Eddie. Let's go get that deer meat from your wagon."

Joe sat cross-legged on his bedroll contemplating the idea of one final pipe before he slept. If he decided to smoke, he would have to walk all the way over to the wagon encampment to borrow the fire to light it, and at the moment he was too relaxed to feel like going anywhere. On the other hand, that last pipe before sleeping was one of life's finer pleasures.

He smiled a little to himself. If this was the worst of his worries . . .

Joe stiffened and moved into a crouch, ready to spring up with knife or tomahawk. Someone was approaching. The night was dark, but he could hear the whisper of feet moving through the grass.

He relaxed again when he saw that his visitor wore a dress.

And he smiled broadly when she came closer and he recognized Fiona McCarthy's slim form.

"Good evening," he said, laying the empty pipe aside and standing.

"Oh, there you are. I knew you were somewhere out here, but I wasn't sure exactly where."

"Is there a problem?" Fiona came close enough that he could have reached out and touched her. But he did not. He ached to take her into his arms and bury his face in the softness of her hair. But he did nothing.

"I wanted . . . I want to ask you if it is dangerous."

"What is?"

"You know. Those Indians. Can they be trusted?"

Joe laughed. "They can be trusted to steal you blind if you turn your back on them. But hurt anyone? No, they won't do that. Were you, uh, wanting something of them?"

"Oh." Fiona's hand went to her throat. "Not . . . not me, no. It is my father. He . . ."

"He went to visit the Ree camp," Joe finished for her. He saw her chin drop as she appeared to concentrate on her toes instead of looking at him.

"Yes," she said in a small voice.

Joe's voice hardened. "He didn't take whiskey to them, did he?"

"No, absolutely not. He . . . the truth is, he doesn't have any more. He drank it all while my mother was . . . you know."

"That's good. That he didn't have any whiskey to give them, that is. Whiskey and Indians don't mix too well and most generally causes trouble."

"He . . . some of the men, that is . . ." She seemed not to know quite how to go on with such an unladylike topic.

"I know. It's all right. Nobody will get hurt if that's all that's worrying you."

"No." Her voice now was no more than a faint whisper barely heard.

"What is it, girl?"

"I wondered . . ." Her chin came up and she moved half a step closer to him. "I wanted to know if you went to the Indian girls too, Joseph. I think it would have broken my heart if you went there too."

Then Fiona was in his arms. She came to him so naturally that he would never be entirely sure just which one of them made that first move toward the other.

He kissed her. Deeply. And ran his hands over the softnesses of her slender body.

He more than half-expected Fiona to cry out or push him away. She did not. Her breath came quicker and she returned his kisses with every bit as much ardor.

Joe picked her up, then knelt and laid her gently onto his blankets.

He lay down beside her.

It was Fiona's hand that went to the buttons of her dress.

✢ 16 ✢

JOE BUMPED THE paint horse into a lope, taking it ahead of the wagon train for more than a mile before he brought the horse to a halt and pulled its head around so that he was looking out across the flat, shallow, sandy course of the Platte. The only thing he was seeking ahead of the train this morning was solitude. He needed time to think, time without the constant interruptions of responsibility.

A virgin! Fiona. Good Lord. She had been a virgin.

Oh, he'd had virgins before this. But they had been Indian girls, offered by their fathers with apology for their unproven state and the clear understanding that the deal for them could be renegotiated if they did not perform adequately.

He had only had to actually do that once. She was a stubborn little Ute girl who wanted nothing to do with any hairy-faced white man. No amount of beating had changed her, and eventually he had taken her back to her uncle. Of course, by then all the trade goods Joe paid for the little bitch had disappeared and the only thing that could be done was to arrange for a replacement. He'd ended up stuck for an entire winter with a fat widow who came into his lodge with four small children in tow. She'd been a good cook, though. And she just plain loved to make the beast with two backs.

Joe smiled now thinking back to that winter. That one was certainly no virgin.

The smile faded. Neither was Fiona McCarthy. Now.

He supposed that should not make any difference. But it did. Fiona was not some trollop who casually passed it around. She was . . . dammit, Fiona was a lady. Never mind any lack of money or position. She was everything a lady was supposed to be. She was gentle and kind and lovely and . . . and he'd taken her without any thought beyond the moment.

And of his feelings for her.

The simple truth was that Joe Moss *did* have feelings for this girl.

She was not the sort of girl to be used and easily discarded afterward.

It was common enough for him to engage in dalliances along the way when he took on a train to guide across the plains. There was generally some daughter or widow or, in truth, some horny wife who was not getting enough in her husband's blankets. But those women meant nothing to him, nothing more than the pleasures of the moment. They were readily enjoyed and easily forgotten.

Fiona . . . oh, Lord, Fiona was different.

He felt . . . Joe did not really know what he felt toward Fiona. He knew that she touched a part of him that had never before been explored. When he looked at Fiona, he felt something stir inside his chest and belly, not only in his groin.

When he looked at her, he wanted to protect her. When

he touched her . . . oh, Lordy, when he touched her, when he tasted her, when he heard the beat of her heart and felt the warmth of her . . .

He got an erection again now from thinking about her, but his feelings for Fiona went far, far beyond physical desire. He wanted . . .

Joe did not know what he wanted from her. Or, more accurately, did not know how much he wanted from her. How far he wanted this thing, whatever it was, to go.

He knew only that he wanted it to continue.

He did not want to hurt her. He would never want that, not in any manner.

But he knew he wanted to be with her again. To have her. To hold and to bed her.

An eggshell once broken can never be made whole again, and a girl once deflowered can never be a virgin again. Twice, thrice, a thousand times coupled would make no difference in that regard. So there really was no reason to avoid being with her—as often as possible—for the rest of the journey west.

But what then? After Joe brought the wagons across the Sierras to the Californias, what then?

He was still sitting there, bemused and uncertain, the paint fidgeting beneath him, when the slow-moving wagons creaked and lumbered their way near and he heard someone call out his name.

Joe had no more answers now than when he'd ridden out in search of them.

He wheeled the paint, careful to avoid looking back along the line for Brendan McCarthy's wagon, and again put the horse into a lope toward the west.

✠ 17 ✠

THE TRAIN WAS moving well. They made a steady eleven or twelve miles each day now that the fevers no longer plagued them. The men were keeping on top of the maintenance for their rigs—something Joe insisted on and frequently checked—and the oxen were holding up well. Joe figured they would take three days' break at Fort Laramie. Laramie was ten days away, he calculated. If nothing went wrong, that is. A man never knew about that. Not really.

Early in the afternoon, he saw a small band of horsemen on the horizon. Indians, he was sure, but too far away for him to see who or what they were.

"Do you see over yonder, Mr. Moss?" Tommy Kramer asked when Joe turned back to join the wagons from his position a quarter mile or so to the front. "Bandits, do you think?"

"Indians more likely," Joe told him.

The boy looked more excited than frightened at the thought.

"Stay close to your mother, Tommy."

"I can take care of myself, Mr. Moss."

"That's why I want you to stay close to your mom. So's you can take care of her." He could see that Tommy was pleased at the responsibility the wagon master gave him.

"I will, Mr. Moss. You can count on me."

"I know I can, son. No need to take up a gun, though. I'll let you know if there might be that sort of trouble."

"Yes, sir. I'll do whatever you say."

Joe touched the wide, drooping brim of his Mexican hat and bumped Tharp's gray horse into a lope back along the train, wanting to head off any excitement.

For the time being.

Indians could be notional, and a man never knew ahead of time what they were apt to do. More than a few of the scars Joe carried on his body had been inflicted by Indians. He'd learned a long time ago not to trust a man to do the Christian thing if he wasn't a Christian. On the other hand, most Indians he'd known could be trusted to keep their word. The trick was to get them to genuinely commit to that word to start with.

By the time he'd made his swing back along the train, the band—a raiding party of some sort, he guessed; a hunting party would have brought a few women or slaves along to do the skinning and butchering, and he saw no females among them—was less than a half mile away, approaching from upriver at a walk.

He went to the head of the train and made sure they saw him hand his rifle to Samuel Kramer before he rode out to meet the Indians. It was an offer of peace. Not that he'd sheathed all of his fangs. There were seven Indians in this bunch, and the rifle could account for only one of them if things went to hell. His horse pistols would be every bit as effective at close range, and his knife and tomahawk never ran out of ammunition. Peaceful gestures were well and good. But Joe was not about to disarm himself. Not for any son of a bitch.

The Indians were southern Cheyenne, he saw by their clothing and accoutrements when he came near them. He greeted them in their own tongue, which near about exhausted his command of that language, then switched to sign language.

The leader of the bunch was young, probably not yet out of his teens, but he was warrior enough to enlist six others to follow him. All but one of the band looked considerably older than the youngster who was leading them. None of them was wearing war paint. Not that that meant so terribly much considering that they had not expected to run into anyone.

They talked for a few minutes; then Joe pointed to the leader and to one other warrior. Those two followed him back to the train while the remaining five dismounted and lay down in the grass.

"What is this?" Sam Kramer asked when Joe and the two Indians reached his wagon.

Translating his words into sign language as he went, Joe said, "This is Young Elk, warrior chief of the southern Cheyenne. This man is Red Ear. They're part of a raiding party out t' steal horses off some Pawnee they heard is out this way. I told them we'd give them a pound o' sugar and a pound o' coffee an' two twists of Virginia tobacca."

"We don't—"

"Just do it, Samuel. I gave my word."

"I see. Well . . . all right then. But I hope . . . I mean,

they are savages, you know. I wouldn't want to encourage them. If you know what I mean."

"Look, just get everybody to chip in when this sorta thing happens, Samuel. That little bit of stuff ain't gonna make anybody starve, not us nor them either one. It's just a friendly thing t' do. If it's the value of the stuff you're worried about, I'll replace it outa my own pocket when we get to Fort Laramie."

"No, don't misunderstand me. I just thought—"

"Come on, Sam. Little coffee, little sugar, little tobacco. That don't mean shit to us an' it keeps them happy. Like I said. Friendly."

"Very well." Kramer disappeared into the back of his wagon, and emerged a minute or so later with the goods Joe promised. He handed them to Joe, who in turn passed them to Young Elk.

"Go in peace, my little brother," he told the youngster in sign language. "I hope you find many horses and have many brave things to tell when you return to your people."

"I will show you my scalps when we meet again, Mankiller," Young Elk said in English.

"You know me?"

"I know you, Mankiller," Young Elk said, still in English.

Joe nodded. "Good luck," he said.

Young Elk wheeled his horse and Red Ear followed on his heels as the two of them went yipping and showing off back to their companions.

Kramer looked at Joe rather nervously. "Mankiller?" he asked. "What was that about?"

"It's just a name I was given by the Indians, that's all."

"I think—"

"Don't fret yourself about it, all right?" Joe snapped, his voice hard and eyes flashing warning signals. "Just . . .

leave it be, Samuel. Leave it the hell alone." He wheeled the gray and headed back down the line of wagons.

Late that evening, Joe lay on his blankets with Fiona soft and warm beside him. The two were sated. For the moment. He knew if he spent the rest of his life trying, he could never get enough of this girl. She stirred him in ways and to degrees that no woman ever had before her.

It startled Joe to realize that. Never in his life had he been one for permanence. Never cared about it. Yet with Fiona, he was having thoughts about exactly that.

He was about to discuss his feelings with her—in itself a remarkable change because he never discussed his deeper feelings with anyone, ever—and opened his mouth to do so, but Fiona spoke first.

"May I ask you something?" Her head lay on his chest; her voice was slightly muffled because she was pressed so tight against him.

"Anything," he assured her, stroking the back of her head.

"I heard something today, something going around among the people."

"What is it?"

"I heard . . . I heard that Indian today called you by a name. A very strange name."

Joe nodded. "Mankiller."

"It's true then?"

"It is what the tribes call me, yes."

Fiona sat up, the moonlight pale on her naked flesh. She was so beautiful, she took Joe's breath away and caused a lump to form in his throat. "Joseph, why would they call you that? It is a terrible name."

He shrugged. "T' tell you the truth, I hardly ever think about it no more. It's just a name."

"But why? How did they come to call you that?"

Joe pulled her back down to his side and smoothed her

hair, then ran his hand across the planes and hollows of her back. "It's a long story."

"Tell me." Fiona pulled away from him and sat up again. "Tell me, Joseph."

He hesitated, afraid he would lose her. But he knew he would not lie to her. Never would he lie to her. "It was a long time ago, Fiona. I hadn't been in the mountains very long. I was riding by myself, me and a saddle horse an' two pack animals carrying trade goods along with what furs I'd already swapped for along the way. A bunch o' Piegans decided they'd ruther rob me of my beads and stuff than to trade me out of it."

He shrugged again. "Prob'ly they didn't have anything to trade with but they wanted some foofaraw to show off. That and a white man's scalp an' those horses. So they waited till I set up for the night an' they jumped me."

"They would have scalped you? For real?"

"That isn't just something you read about in magazines, Fiona. I reckon it's real enough." He could have fetched the pack he carried in Samuel Kramer's trailer and showed her some examples of Indian scalps, but suspected a gentle girl like Fiona would not much appreciate them.

"They would have killed you then," she said, not as a question.

"It's what they had in mind, yeah."

"Is that . . . I mean, these scars . . . is that when you got them?" She traced the marks on his body with the flat of her hand.

"I reckon I got some of them then."

"And the Indians. What happened to them?"

"There was six of them. I shot one. Broke another's skull with the butt of my rifle. Grabbed up his tomahawk . . . this 'hawk here, it was," he said, touching the handle of the weapon that was never out of reach. "I took it up and went to swinging it. It was dark and there was enough of them t' get in each other's way. Me, I didn't have to worry about who I could chop or who I oughtn't. They was all enemies, so I just laid into them. Time it was all over, there was four dead and one bad hurt. One of them got away. That one was hurt, but not too awful bad. I heard him ride off. It was him that talked about what happened that night. I don't know if it was him or someone he told it to that started in to calling me Mankiller after that. The name got around. Now, like I said, it's just a name they call me by."

Fiona lay back down at his side, but he could feel a stiffness in her body and her eyes were wide open, glistening in what little light there was from the moon and the distant stars. After several minutes she asked, "Only one got away?"

"That's right."

"Then what happened to the one you said was badly wounded?"

"He was still alive when I rode outa there in the morning. I never went back t' see if he lived or not." That warrior's scalp was among those in Kramer's wagon. But Joe did not intend to mention that to Fiona. Not that he would lie about it. If she ever asked him if he scalped that Indian, he would tell her. Until or unless she asked, though, he could see no reason to bring it up.

"That is terrible, Joseph."

"Terrible that I killed those Piegans?"

"No. I'm glad you did that. They would have killed you. I think it is terrible that they attacked you like that."

Joe shrugged and laid his hand on Fiona's bare back. He could feel a stirring of renewed arousal. She must have seen or sensed it somehow. Her hand went to him, holding him lightly while she began to kiss his chest.

Fiona's body was no longer tight with tension, and he

guessed she had come to terms with the name the Indians gave him.

He reached for her, pressed her onto her back, and began to move over her, only to be interrupted by a high-pitched scream that came from the direction of the night's encampment.

✦ 18 ✦

IT WAS OVER by the time Joe got there, wearing only his trousers, tomahawk in hand and still trying to hastily button his fly. A clutch of women were gathered amid some cattails beside the riverbank. Several men stood on dry ground nearby.

Joe resisted an impulse to glance behind to see if Fiona was following. He had told her to get dressed and circle around to enter the camp from another direction so no one would realize they had been together, but he did not know if she would obey or not.

There was little moonlight, but his eyes were acclimated to the darkness so he could see well enough to know that something was very seriously wrong here. One of the Harvey girls, the oldest of the four, he thought, although they all had very much the same appearance. This one was called Millicent, he thought. Milly for short. She was sixteen or thereabouts.

The women were gathered around Milly like a clutch of

hens gabbling over an injured chick. They seemed to have wrapped her in a blanket or some such and several of them were hugging her. Milly herself was weeping. He could see her shoulders shudder and tremble.

Joe waded into the near-stagnant water of the little pond or eddy where the cattails grew. "What's the trouble, ladies? Did she see a bear or somethin'?" Joe knew damned good and well she could not have seen a bear or any other wild thing big enough to harm her. Not here she couldn't. But you never know what a frightened young'un will *think* they see.

"She was . . . I can't tell you what the problem is," Mrs. Craddock told him.

"Ma'am, I need t' know what's happened here to get this child so upset. I got to if I want t' keep the folks in the company safe."

A couple of the other women glanced over toward the men standing on the riverbank close by.

"Would it be easier for you t' tell me in confidence? Private like?" Joe asked.

Mrs. Craddock nodded.

"Then let's you and me go over here where we won't be overheard. Would that be better?"

"Yes. Please."

Joe took the lady by the elbow and guided her onto dry ground, then several rods upstream. The other ladies, he noticed, began shooing the menfolk away and leading Millicent Harvey out of the water and on toward her family's wagon. They were carrying her almost as much as leading her, he noticed.

"Now then," he said when he was sure no one could listen in on the conversation. "What happened t' that child?"

"She was . . . she was . . . how can I put this delicately, Mr. Moss?"

"She was assaulted?" he suggested.

Mrs. Craddock nodded.

"In a man-an'-woman sort of way?" he guessed.

"Yes. Yes, she was. She was . . . she said she wanted to bathe. She thought she would not be seen. Because of the rushes, you understand."

"But somebody seen her go in there?" Joe asked.

"Yes. Exactly. He . . . followed her. Grabbed her from behind, she said, and put his hand over her mouth so she could not cry out. Then he . . . hurt her." Mrs. Craddock paused. "I don't want to say what . . . you know."

"It's all right. You don't hafta tell me no details, ma'am. There's things I ruther not know. For the girl's sake, you understand."

Mrs. Craddock bobbed her head in agreement. "Thank you. Milly is such a dear girl. Very shy and gentle. She is just horribly embarrassed by all of this."

"Yes, ma'am. I'd guess she must've got a look at whoever hurt her, though, didn't she."

"She says . . . she says it was dark. She was afraid for her life. She says she is not sure who did . . . that . . . to her."

"Uh-huh. Did she say what he was wearing?"

"I don't think I asked her. Don't think any of us did. Why would that matter, Mr. Moss?"

"It probably don't. I was just curious," he lied with a smile. "Thank you for bein' straight with me, Miz Craddock. Now let's go see if Millicent is up t' telling me anything about this fella."

"All right, but I don't think she would want to say very much about it. Certainly not to a man. Any man."

"Yes, ma'am. Perhaps you could ask her for me then? I'd like to know what he was wearing. And ma'am, I don't mean t' make things any the more uncomfortable for the child, but I got to ask. Did this man, uh, did he finish what he come out there for? Did he actually rape her an' not just scare her?"

"Yes, Mr. Moss. The man who attacked Milly took her virginity from her. He ruined her, Mr. Moss."

"Yes, ma'am," Joe said, although he might not have agreed that the girl was ruined. Hurt, yes. Deflowered, sure. But ruined? Not in body. It was too soon to judge how something like this would affect her mind. But he would not necessarily agree that the girl was ruined. "Let's find Milly and the other ladies an' you can see will she tell you what I want t' know."

"This way, Mr. Moss. The Harvey wagon is right over here."

Two of the women were standing at the back of the wagon. The rest were inside with the girl. Joe could see moving shadows faint on the thick canvas wagon cover, but could not see or hear what was going on inside. "I'll wait here, ma'am, while you go an' talk with her if y' please."

The wait probably seemed longer than it really was. It felt like an interminable passage of time, but probably was not more than five or six minutes. Too long to Joe's mind, but there was nothing he could do to speed things along. When she did come back, Mrs. Craddock was grim-faced and angry.

"She says she does not know who the man was, Mr. Moss. She was very clear on that point."

"Yes, ma'am."

"He was dressed in trousers. With galluses. She was sure about that."

"All right. What else?"

"Else? That is all she remembers, Mr. Moss. That's it."

Joe struggled to control his impatience. If he could just go and talk to the damn girl himself . . . He could not, of course. She would close up complete if he, a man and a relative stranger at that, tried to question her about something so very personal and private. "Miz Craddock, did the man have a beard? Mustache? What color was his hair? Is there anything else at all she could say about him?"

"I . . . I could ask again, I suppose."

"Please, ma'am. Please." Joe figured he had to be prepared for another wait. Dammit. Because by now the fellow had had more than enough time to change clothes.

Joe had hoped to find him by spotting whoever was walking around in wet britches. A fellow who is humping a girl in shallow water is going to get himself awfully wet. And so too with the pants that would be down around his ankles while he is in the saddle with the girl. This man who raped Millicent Harvey had to have come out of the water soaking wet from the waist down. But with time enough to change clothes and dry himself off, it was going to be mighty hard for Joe to figure out who the rapist in this company was.

Ten minutes later, he approached Thomas Harvey and asked could he borrow the man's lantern.

"Whatever for?" Harvey wanted to know.

"So's I can find the man that's gone and hurt your daughter, Thomas."

"With a lantern?"

Joe nodded. "Yes, sir. If you'll give me the borrow of it."

"Take it, Moss. Take anything that I have if you think it will lead you to him."

Joe lifted Harvey's lantern down off the tailgate of his wagon and started poking his head and shoulders inside the other wagons in the train and never mind niceties like privacy and such shit.

✛ 19 ✛

"WHICH O' YOU owns these britches?" Joe demanded of the men who were assembled in a tight, angry knot well apart from the Harvey wagon, where the women were clucking and fluttering around Millicent.

It surprised Joe not at all that no one admitted ownership of the trousers.

"These came out of one o' the bachelor wagons," he said in a firm voice. There were three rigs in the train transporting men traveling without families, men who more than likely intended to hunt for gold when they reached the Californias or who wanted to establish themselves in the West before sending for wives and families they left back wherever they came from. Joe knew good and well that some—a good many—of those would never get around to sending for those they'd left behind. Those men looked on the West as a chance to start over. Without encumbrances.

"What about them?" James Fenn asked. "They look ordinary enough to me."

"These britches are wet, Jim. Wet with river water. I run my thumb over them an' come up with grit from the river an' slime from around the base o' cattails. These here britches, Jim, belong to the man that raped little Milly Harvey."

In fact, all Joe could tell about them was that they were indeed wet. The grit and the slime were pure booshwah intended to spook the owner of the trousers into thinking he had already been caught.

"Which bachelor wagon, Moss?" someone demanded.

"Adams," Joe said.

That caused a general shuffling about as the men peered at whoever was standing next to them, trying to see if there was a suspect nearby. The wagon in question was occupied by four fellows—none of them gentlemen—from New Hampshire: Quincy Adams, who claimed to be related to the past presidents who were similarly named; Albert Benedict, a farmer; George Tarleton; and Randolph Simonson. The four were sometimes quarrelsome among themselves, but had caused no trouble with the other emigrants, at least none that had reached Joe's ears.

"Well, I'm right here," Quincy Adams said, "and I've done nothing to that girl. Those pants are not mine."

Simonson stepped forward and said, "Let me see those, will you?"

Joe handed the wet trousers over and Simonson inspected them. "I will tell you straight out, Moss, that these look like a pair of pants I washed this afternoon and hung on the lazy-board of our rig, but those were most about dry by the time I went to play cards with Kuntzler and them. And I did not harm that child."

Ray Kuntzler moved to the front of the crowd and put in, "I can back that up, Moss. Randy was there with us from before nightfall till we heard the commotion about the girl. We ate, had us a few drinks, and was all together right up until the time we walked over here to see what was going on. There's no way Randy could've done it, pants or no pants."

"What about Benedict and Tarleton then?" Joe asked. "Could one of them have grabbed your clean pants this evening?"

"I'm right here, Moss," Benedict said from the back of the crowd. "And I didn't take his pants. I got pants of my own."

"Tarleton? Is George Tarleton here?" Joe asked. "No?" he said after a moment. "Has anybody seen Tarleton?"

"I seen him this evening," Ed Thompson put in. "He had a jug in his hand and he was . . . well, shit. Come to think of it, he was walking upstream toward that stand of cattails."

"Anybody see him since then?" Joe asked.

No one answered.

"All right then. I want you all to search through the camp. Look into the wagons. Under them. Everywhere. When you find Tarleton, bring him back here. We'll get some straight answers from him before we decide anything else," Joe told them. "But mind that we don't know for sure that he done this thing. He might be laying up drunk somewhere and not know nothing about any of it."

"If he did do it, he'd best watch his ass."

"I'd like to get my licks in on him," another voice injected.

"If he did, we must give him a fair hearing," Samuel Kramer cautioned. "We mustn't go flying off the handle until we know for sure what happened."

"All right then. Find Tarleton," Joe said. "And bring him back here."

The men dispersed quickly, disappearing into the night. The women were still crowded close around the Harvey wagon, where Milly was being comforted and looked after.

Joe caught a glimpse of Fiona as he headed toward the cattails where the crime was committed. He wished he could hold her now and reassure himself that she was all right, but of course he could not. Not with everyone watching.

He reached the spot where Milly and the ladies had been when he first saw them. He waded into the cold, shallow water. Once he got away from the bank, it was easy enough to find the spot where the girl was attacked. A clump of cattails were crushed and broken where she had been thrown down. Close by, he found a piece of flour sacking draped over some of the rushes, probably put there by the girl to use as a towel when she was done bathing.

The sign at that spot was broad enough for a blind man to follow. But it was not the only sign that was left.

Joe could easily see where Milly had walked into the water, and he could see also where someone approached her from the river side of the shallow backwater. That would have been the attacker. Tarleton presumably, although he did not know that for sure.

Joe followed the trail of very slightly bent cattails back and found a place where someone had crouched in hiding.

Dammit to hell, he thought, the son of a bitch might still have been there when Milly's cries brought everyone to the bank. From there he must have slipped back onto dry ground and snuck in among the wagons while everyone else was distracted by news of the rape.

He would have had plenty of time to change into dry trousers and . . . and what? Joe wondered. Would he try to brazen it out by denying he was the rapist? Or . . .

Joe knew damn good and well if he had been the one to commit so heinous a crime, he would want to get the hell away. And fast.

George Tarleton did not own a horse, and no one was going to run very far or very fast in a wagon drawn by oxen.

For that matter, the wagon wasn't even his. It belonged to Quincy Adams.

No, if he was in Tarleton's place, Joe figured he would . . .

"Shit," he mumbled aloud.

Then he turned and began trotting out toward where he'd laid out his small camp. And where he had left his paint and the gray horse hobbled.

Moss cursed, his facial expression hard and the look in his eyes lethal. The son of a bitch had stolen Tharp's gray. And Joe's saddle. And, dammit, the rifle that he'd left lying beside his bed when Milly's cries took him at a run toward the encampment.

Tarleton had not taken the paint. Or perhaps had not been able to ride or steal it. The paint horse was a fractious son of a bitch and did not take easily to being handled by strangers.

Joe quickly dressed. He had run to the wagons wearing only his trousers and carrying the tomahawk. Now he took a moment to slip into his moccasins and pull his shirt on. He draped the usual pouches and bags over his shoulders, and wrapped his sash in place with the pistols and bowie knife along with his tomahawk, then picked up the broad-brimmed Mexican hat.

The paint nickered and nudged Joe with its muzzle when he approached it. Quickly, he tied a loop of strong cord around its jaw Indian-fashion as a substitute for bridle and bit, then removed the hobbles. With a bound, he mounted the paint bareback and sat there for a moment thinking.

There was no way to track a horse and rider at night. Hell, on open prairie, there was very little chance of tracking one horse in daylight. What he needed to do was to figure out which way Tarleton would try to flee.

Certainly, the man had not ridden back into or close to the wagon camp, and it was not likely that he would try to cross the treacherous Platte at night on a strange horse. There was nothing to the south except miles and miles of nothing but miles and miles. Surely, Tarleton could escape in that direction, but he would not know how to fend for himself there, not knowing where to find water and with only one charge of powder and ball in the rifle, for Joe's bullet pouch and powder horn were dangling from a stout thong across his chest. Tarleton had not taken those when he grabbed up the rifle.

Tarleton could ride west to Fort Laramie if he chose. But he did not know this country and probably would not want to travel it alone.

No, Joe thought, the likely route would be for him to turn back east. Toward Missouri and civilization. That would be especially appealing since the wagons were rolling westward and every day of travel would put more distance between Tarleton and the emigrant company.

The man very likely then would first ride south, probably for a fair good number of miles, then turn east and angle northward to pick up the Platte. After that all he would have to do would be to backtrack the wagon trail through country he already knew and would be reasonably comfortable with.

Joe grunted. If he took the paint and rode straight back along the river, he should be able to get ahead of Tarleton and be waiting for him when the fugitive returned to the Platte.

Joe wheeled the horse east and put his heels to it.

✥ 20 ✥

JOE SAT WITH his back propped against the bole of a cottonwood tree. The sun was up, had been long enough to put some warmth into the air and for Joe to use his burning glass to light a pipe. He sat with his arms draped over his knees, enjoying the taste of the smoke and the quiet of the morning. He had not particularly noticed before just how noisy and hectic life was in the vicinity of the wagon train. This was a pleasant change.

The only sounds he could hear were the twitter of some birds, the rustle of leaves overhead, and the bubbly sizzling sound of tobacco burning in his pipe.

The only thing he could see in the distance was the grass that extended across the vast plains and the silently moving shadows as a handful of small, puffy clouds drifted high above.

Joe grunted softly to himself.

He could see the grass, yes, and the shadows. And now there was a small dark dot that had come into view and was moving slowly from west to east. Coming very gradually closer too.

Joe finished his pipe and tapped it against the cotton-wood to knock the dottle out. He took his time replacing the hot pipe in the pouch where it belonged, then stood and stretched for a moment to work out a few kinks before he made his way deeper into the grove. He clucked once to alert the paint to his presence.

When he reached the horse, he untied it from the sapling where it had been secured and once again fastened a loop around its jaw, the cord positioned in the flat gap behind the paint's teeth. The single rein worked quite well as a bit once both horse and rider became accustomed to it. The Indians, having no metal, had used the method for generations.

Joe rubbed the animal's poll and ran his fingers through its mane like a comb, then took a moment to inspect each hoof. He was in no hurry. He had time.

Finally, he backed away far enough to let him take a long, quick stride and bound onto the paint's back. He guided the horse to the edge of the grove where he'd been waiting and looked to the south again.

Tharp's gray was still a hundred yards or so away and moving toward the river where Joe sat watching.

Joe waited until George Tarleton almost reached the eastern end of the grove, probably expecting to water the gray there and take a rest in the shade himself. Then Joe kneed the paint forward, slipping through the trees so that he emerged directly in front of Tarleton and less than a rod distant from him.

Tarleton was startled. The man yanked back on the reins so hard the gray almost sat back onto its butt before it recovered and angrily shook itself.

"Jesus! Moss. You oughtn't to scare a fellow like that."

Tarleton tried to smile, but the effort found no success. He only managed to make his lips twitch nervously.

"Now I'm real sorry, George. I never meant t' put a fright in you."

"No, it isn't that. You just . . . I, uh, I just wasn't expecting you. You know?"

"Oh yeah, George, I know." Joe applied pressure with his right calf, easing the paint sideways to its left. Away from the muzzle of the rifle that lay wedged between George Tarleton's lap and the pommel of the saddle, Joe's saddle. "You weren't expecting to see anyone from the company again, were you?"

"I, uh, look, Moss, I can explain all this. It isn't like you think."

"What isn't like I think, George?" Joe nudged the paint a little closer to the gray.

"The . . . that girl. It was her, Moss. She wanted it. Hell, she's the one propositioned me. She only let out that yell 'cause she heard somebody comin' toward us. She didn't want to be found doing what, uh, what we was doing. You know how it is, Moss. It was all her idea."

"Oh, I know how that is, George, but that would be between you an' the other folks in the company, wouldn't it?"

"Yeah, I, uh . . . yeah."

"I didn't ask you about Milly, though, did I, George?"

"I guess you didn't at that, Joe." Tarleton again gave him a rather tentative and nervous smile that flickered on and off several times over and finally died. "Then if it ain't the girl you come down here about, Joe, just what, uh . . ."

"I don't exactly know how this escaped your mind, George, but that's my horse you're setting on." Joe began to get his blood up; he began to loosen the control he'd been keeping over himself. "You stole my horse, you son of a fucking *bitch!*" He was shouting by the end of that.

Tarleton was startled all over again. He lifted the rifle off his lap and began to swing the barrel around to point toward Joe.

Joe let out an ear-shattering scream, an Indian war cry calculated to frighten enemies into immobility, and drove his heels hard into the sides of the paint.

The horse leaped forward, straight for George Tarleton and the gray.

Tarleton tried frantically to bring the rifle to bear, but before he could do so Joe was upon him. Tarleton's hand clutched convulsively at the rifle. He squeezed down and the weapon accidentally discharged, the ball flying harmlessly toward the far riverbank.

Joe ignored both the rifle and the pistols in his sash. He grabbed Tarleton by the throat and leaped off the paint, yanking Tarleton to the ground with him. The rifle clattered useless on the ground and the gray horse bolted into a short run, but quickly stopped lest it get too far away from the paint, whose company meant the security of a herd.

The two men hit the ground hard. The air was driven out of Joe's lungs by the impact, but he kept his hold on Tarleton's throat.

"You cocksucker!" Joe came to his knees, looming over Tarleton, who lay on his back with his eyes wide and panicky. Tarleton grabbed Joe's wrist with both hands and tried to pull Joe's hand off his neck.

"You son of a bitch," Joe hissed.

His blood was up and he was within half a second of squeezing the life out of George Tarleton.

But no, dammit. Milly Harvey deserved to see this bastard die. Killing him now would be too easy on him.

Joe eased his hold a little and pulled Tarleton to a sitting position.

"If you got a knife or a pocket gun on you, you prick, go

ahead an' use it. If you can." He let go of the man's throat and stood, shaking from the rush of battle lust. "Try me, you bastard. I hope you will."

Tarleton gulped for air. He was rubbing his throat with both hands. His complexion was pale except for patches of bright red where Joe had taken hold of him. It took him three tries to get any sound out so he could respond.

"God! Don't hurt me, Moss. I . . . I would've sent money. For your horse. I was gonna do that. Really. I intended to right off. You got to believe me, Moss. I wasn't gonna steal that horse. I just meant to borrow him. I . . . you know how it is. I knew people wouldn't understand. About that girl, I mean. It was her all along, Joe. She wanted it. Near about waved her puss under my nose, Joe. That . . . that wasn't my fault. None of it. But try an' tell that to a bunch of stupid sheep like them women. I knew . . . soon as that flirty little bitch yelled, I knew I was in the shit. You know? They wouldn't of believed me. So I grabbed your horse an' skeedaddled. But I was gonna pay for him. I swear I was. I was gonna send money first chance I got."

"Are you sure you don't want t' pull a knife? Or anything?" Joe had control of himself now. His breathing was back to normal, and the heat that had been in his blood was replaced now with an icy calm.

"Joe, I . . . no, man, I wouldn't do nothing like that. You and me, we been friends."

Friends? Joe barely knew the man. And damn sure did not want to.

"Then get your sorry ass up, Tarleton. Get up an' get back on that gray. And let me tell you something. Any time you take a notion to run again, you're welcome t' do exactly that. Me and the paint are gonna be right behind. You hear what I'm saying, Tarleton? I won't mind even a little if you want t' make a break for it."

"I wouldn't do nothing like that, Joe. Where, uh, where are you taking me? It's an awful long way to the nearest judge or anything."

"We're going back to the train, Tarleton. And don't you worry about facing a judge someplace. I am gonna be your judge. The men of the emigrant company are gonna be your jury. You are gonna get a fair trial, Tarleton. I'll see to that. Then when your trial is done, I figure to cut your dick off and leave you to bleed to death. Figure that'd be a fair punishment for a rapist." There was not a hint of mirth in Joe's smile. "Don't you think so, George?"

"God, Joe, you can't be serious about that. You can't. It ain't human to treat a man like that. You wouldn't really do that, Joe. Would you?"

Joe did not answer. He picked up the rein of the paint and collected his rifle from the ground where Tarleton had dropped it. He also made sure George Tarleton was watching when he carefully reloaded the rifle.

Then he leaped onto the paint and with the muzzle of his rifle motioned for Tarleton to mount the gray.

"Move it, you piece of shit."

Tarleton moved it. With alacrity.

Bringing George Tarleton into the wagon encampment was close akin to kicking an anthill. And these ants were the kind that wanted to bite.

As soon as folks saw that Joe had his prisoner, they came rushing, but not so much to greet as for an opportunity to vilify.

Anyone who had the impression that only Indian squaws were vicious in their treatment of prisoners would have quickly learned an ugly truth had they seen the way these respectable white women clamored for Tarleton's blood.

For his part, Tarleton was terrified. Damn well had the right to be too, in Joe's opinion. The ladies would likely have ripped the man's balls off if they had the chance. Joe was quite frankly more than a little surprised by the language some of them used too. He wouldn't have thought they even knew words like that, much less that they would be willing to use them.

"My God, Moss, you got to protect me," Tarleton

bleated, reining the gray horse so tight against the side of the paint that Joe thought he was trying to crawl onto the back of the paint with him. "Please."

"Let us through, ladies. Everything's under control now. Let us get past, please."

Joe kneed the paint into a trot, the horse's broad chest bumping several of the women aside before they got the idea that he was going to ride through them whether they got out of his way or not. After that, he had a clear path to the river and to the Harvey wagon.

"Thomas," Joe called. "Are you in there?"

Thomas Harvey stuck his head out past the closed flap at the back of his rig.

"Tell your daughter we have the man that hurt her. She's welcome to see him punished if she's of a mind to. Doesn't have to, o' course, but she's welcome."

Harvey disappeared inside the wagon, then returned a moment later. By that time, the men of the train were beginning to gather around Joe and Tarleton. They did not look any more welcoming than the women had, although they were somewhat more orderly in their expressions of disapproval, or at least less physical about it. They were also much more practiced in their choices of wording when they shouted dire warnings at the prisoner. Like their wives and daughters, though, the gentlemen returned again and again to the basic theme that George Tarleton should be castrated. And as painfully as possible.

"She don't want to lay eyes on him ever again, Moss," Harvey said when he emerged from the back of his wagon.

"What do we do now, Joe?" Samuel Kramer asked amid all the commotion. "Where do we turn for justice?"

"Quiet down, folks," Joe said. "Let me lay this out for you. There's no law out here but what we carry with us. Out here only law is the gun an' the knife an' the rope." Joe turned his attention to Harvey again. "Thomas, I got to ask you a painful thing. I got to ask you t' make sure, an' I mean damn sure, that George Tarleton here is the man that hurt your little girl. You got to ask it of her outright or get her mama t' do it if you can't, but the question has t' be asked and it has t' be answered in plain terms. Once we decide this man is guilty, there's no changing anybody's mind on it for by then it will be too late. And gents, there ain't no way to apologize to a corpse. You got to get it right the first time. Go on now, Thomas. Talk t' your daughter an' to your wife. Then step down an' tell us all what they say."

Harvey withdrew behind the dust-grimed canvas flap, and the men pressed closer around Joe and Tarleton as if they expected the prisoner to bolt for freedom. By then the ladies had caught up, and were gathered in a ring outside the crowd of their menfolk.

There was a moment of silence while everyone waited for Thomas Harvey to emerge from his wagon again. Into that silence Tarleton snarled, "You bastard, Moss, you got no right to judge me for enjoying a little pussy. You're getting all you want from that snooty McCarthy bitch. You don't know—"

The man did not get a chance to complete whatever it was he wanted to say. Joe swung the rifle in a backhanded sweep that caught Tarleton full in the face. Something broke in there and blood sprayed into the air as Tarleton toppled off the gray and fell heavily to the ground underneath the feet of the gray.

A horse will almost turn itself inside out in an effort to avoid stepping on a human being or any other soft object. The gray ducked sideways, knocking down Kramer and two other men in order to avoid stamping on Tarleton. Aaron Zeiss, the blacksmith, grabbed the gray by the cheek-piece and held on to bring it back under control.

Joe kicked his leg over the paint's withers and dropped to the ground beside Tarleton.

"That's your second mistake o' the day, little man."

"You can't—"

"Shut up." Joe kicked him in the belly. He would have aimed for the cods, except Tarleton was curled up into a tight ball trying to protect them from the attentions of some of the others, who had already gotten a few kicks in. Tarleton shut up.

Some of the younger men and older boys crept close and also aimed a few ineffectual kicks at the man. Tarleton was openly weeping by then. His face was streaked with dirt and tears. The treatment was a high price for a piece of ass, but Tarleton had been free to roll the dice. He'd lost.

Thomas Harvey came out of his wagon and climbed down to the ground.

"Well, Thomas?" Samuel Kramer asked. "What do they say?"

"She says . . . Milly says he is the one. She was ashamed to say much before now. She thought he would not be punished for doing this awful thing."

"She is certain?"

"She's sure of it, Sam. There was enough light that she could see him plain when he . . . you know . . . when he was close . . . like that."

Kramer nodded, then turned to Joe. "What do we do now? We have no cage to lock him in. We could tie him, no? Tie him night and day? What do you think?"

"That ain't the way it'll go out here, Samuel. For something serious like this, there's only one sentence. That's death."

"No-o-o-o-o-o-o!" Tarleton wailed. Kramer's son Tommy kicked him again.

"But how . . . who . . . ?"

"I'll take care of it," Joe said calmly.

"You bastard!" Tarleton shouted. Joe ignored him.

"What you folks need t' tell me," Joe said, "is whether the man dies quick or slow."

"What do you mean?"

"I can execute him like a white man an' hang him, or I can do it Indian-style an' start in to skin him. If I do that, he'll die by an' by. But nice and slow."

Kramer went pale at the thought. Rather predictably, in Joe's opinion, a number of the women shouted their votes that Tarleton should die a slow death Indian-style, but the men and a minority of the ladies opted for a quick death by hanging.

"Tie his hands and feet then," Joe said, "and somebody please give me the borrow of a hank o' rope."

Tarleton fought like a wildcat, but all that did was to give the men an excuse to kick and pummel him some more. He was battered and bloody by the time the press of attackers wore him down enough that they could truss him hand and foot.

Willing hands carried him to the nearest tree. It was not much of a tree. But it would do.

A small boy shinnied up the trunk and draped a rope over a fork about fifteen feet up.

"Does anybody know how to tie a hangman's knot?" Joe asked loudly. No one did. Nor did he. He shrugged and fashioned a simple loop in one end of the rope.

"We don't have any way to drop him so we'll put a bunch o' you on the other end. When I give you the nod, drag him up. I'll tie off the end after you get him up there."

"Oh God, God, you can't do this. Please, God, don't do this to me." Tarleton was blubbering and bawling. Snot ran down his face, and a dark blotch showed on the front of his trousers where he'd pissed himself.

Joe stepped forward and secured the loop of rope loosely around Tarleton's throat, then took out his knife and appeared to be fiddling with the noose somehow.

Tarleton screamed, then fainted.

Joe kind of doubted that any of these peaceful, civilized folks realized that he'd just taken George Tarleton's scalp. He slipped the scrap of flesh and hair inside his shirt, then stepped back and nodded. "Pull away, gentlemen, pull away."

Tarleton was able to scream one more time before he was lifted off his feet.

✢ 22 ✢

No one was in any mood to hitch up and travel for the remaining hours of daylight, so Kramer passed the word that they would spend one more night at this site even though very little usable wood was available.

It occurred to Joe that it was time for the emigrants to sling "possum bellies" underneath their wagons. While they walked alongside their wagons each day, they could pick up clumps of whatever dried dung they saw and toss them onto the hammocklike canvas or leather possum bellies for use as fuel.

Buffalo chips were the best for that purpose, being two or three times as large as cow manure, but the dung of almost any of the large grazing animals would burn well enough to heat water or to cook a meal.

He would give them a talk about that this evening, he figured. It would give them something to think about other than George Tarleton.

He took his two horses out to his usual solitary campsite

and hobbled the paint. He turned the paint loose to graze, then stripped the saddle and bridle off the gray and picked up its feet one by one to check them over. He did not know how hard the gray had been used during Tarleton's escape attempt, but it appeared to have come through without harm. He hobbled and loosed it too so it could join the paint on the sparse grass here.

Joe flipped an edge of his blanket over the lock of the rifle placed beside his bedroll to protect it from moisture in case there was dew, then settled into a comfortable cross-legged position to enjoy his pipe while he waited for dusk and time to join the Kramer family for supper. That comfort, though, was confined to the purely physical. Inside, he was in turmoil.

He ached to see Fiona, to hold and to touch her, but he could not. Thanks to that son of a bitch Tarleton, he would not even be able to approach or to speak with her in broad daylight with the members of the company right there beside them.

Why did that bastard have to open his fat mouth and say what he said about Joe and Fiona? Everyone had heard. They might or might not pay attention to it, but they surely had heard. It would not be possible for Joe to speak with Fiona in public at all now. And it might not be possible for him to see her in private either.

There had been women among those who gathered when the rapist was brought in. They too had heard what was said. Would they say hurtful things to Fiona or shun her? God, he hoped not. He would rather cut off his right arm than hurt Fiona McCarthy in any way. And he'd do the cutting himself, damn it.

But, oh, if he could no longer see her . . .

Joe Moss was not a man much given to grieving, and he had learned to avoid any outward show of pain or emotion when under duress. But now, his face twisted in anguish and he squeezed his eyes tight shut and willed himself to let her go. For her sake. But . . . He could not. The thought was too much to bear.

To be without the touch of her hand. The warmth of her presence. To be without the feel of her body next to his. Never to hear her voice or see the moonlight shimmer on her hair as she brushed it. No! He could not bear that punishment.

Yet to continue with her was to risk hurting her. Women could be catty bitches. They would rip her with claws of meanness and flay her with the fangs of their words.

He . . . she . . . could refute Tarleton's accusation by demonstrating that the two of them, Joe and Fiona, had no contact with one another. None. That would put the matter to rest. Not soon perhaps, but eventually.

Joe grimaced. That was a solution so easily seen but so very difficult to apply.

He honestly did not know how he could remain so close to her as this train completed its journey and yet remain apart from her.

He loved her, dammit. It was as simple as that. After all these years, Joe Moss was ensnared in the trap of love.

It was an emotion that was quite frankly new to him. Always he had enjoyed women. Hell, he even enjoyed their company when they had their clothes on. Most of the time. And he'd had . . . he could not begin to remember how many women he'd happily fucked.

He'd had wives of his own—winter wives whose services he bought for a season and then parted from without a second thought—and the wives of other men as well. He'd had red women, white ones, black and brown as well. Once he'd had a screamingly torrid night with the mousy little wife of a missionary. Mousy-looking, that is. She'd been a wild one when he hair came down. Women liked Joe and he liked them right back.

But with all those women and all those years, he never once had felt the things inside him that he felt with Fiona. Never felt his belly turn over and clench tight just from seeing her walk by, his breath coming quick and his heart pounding. Never felt so alive at the simplest touch. Never wanted to hold and protect any woman. Until now.

And now, thanks to that asshole Tarleton, he had to pretend indifference when Fiona was near. If they could just be together at night. On his blankets. If he could work that out . . .

If he could think of a way to do it, he would kill that shit-eater all over again, cut him down and kill him again. But slow this time. If he had the chance to do it over, he would kill Tarleton in the slow and terrible Indian manner.

Joe brooded through the rest of the afternoon, and at supper pretended that all was well.

"What about that man?" Samuel Kramer asked once when his wife stepped away to fetch the coffeepot. "You haven't said anything about burying him. Shouldn't we at least give him a Christian burial?"

"You can do whatever you're of a mind to, Sam. It won't make no difference to me nor to him. I intend t' take him down, though. That rope is near new and it'd be a shame to just leave it there. I want t' get it back to its rightful owner, but I thought I'd wait until dark t' let him down."

"And Tarleton? What will you do with Tarleton after you retrieve the rope?"

Joe shrugged. "Figured I'd just roll him into the river. It's running high enough to float him away. Figure he don't deserve no proper burial, not after what he done."

"Don't . . . please don't do that."

"You want I should leave him there? That rope belongs to Jonas Farge. I'd like to get it back to him."

"Very well. Take, uh, George . . . take George down and return the rope to Jonas, but don't dump the, uh, the body into the river. Leave him there. I'll get some of the others to help me. We will bury him in the morning before we leave."

"All right, fair enough if that's what you want. It really don't make any difference to me."

Joe had an after-supper pipe with Kramer while he waited for night, then excused himself and walked to the riverbank where George Tarleton's body dangled a few feet off the ground. It had been hanging somewhat higher when they first strung him up there, but the constant weight was slowly stretching the rope. That was all right, though. A rope is best after the newness has been stretched out of it anyway.

Joe knocked his pipe against the trunk of the hanging tree, then replaced it into his pouch before he gave his attention to the knot that tied off the free end of the rope.

While he was occupied with that, he heard footsteps behind him.

And a rush toward his back.

Joe wheeled, crouching, to meet whatever attack this was.

✢ 23 ✢

JOE DUCKED AND a dark man-shape went hurdling over him. The fellow's knee banged hard into Joe's shoulder as he flew past, nearly knocking Joe off his feet. The other man landed awkwardly. Joe could hear that his breath was driven out of him with a sound like a drawn-out cough.

Joe whirled, the big bowie flashing in his hand as he sprang at his attacker before the fellow could get his wind back. Joe grabbed a handful of hair and yanked the man's head back.

All that was needed was one quick, deep slash across the throat, then another in the opposite direction. It would be wonderfully efficient. Kill the son of a bitch and take his scalp in damn near the same motion. Joe's hand was already moving to deliver that first deadly slash when he realized who it was who'd jumped him.

"Jesus!" Joe yelped, drawing the knife back and coming swiftly to his feet.

Brendan McCarthy clutched his throat and rolled over and over, writhing on the ground and groaning loudly.

Joe had come within a heartbeat of slaughtering Fiona's father, and wouldn't that be a splendid way to go a-courting. It was a plan not exactly calculated to win the girl's heart.

"What the hell's the matter with you?" Joe demanded as soon as Brendan quit gagging and wallowing around on the ground. "I'd of kilt you, McCarthy, if I didn't see who you was."

Brendan sat up and shook his head. He seemed to still be having trouble getting his breath back. "I damn sure figured to kill *you,* Moss, you son of a bitch."

"You oughtn't to call me that, McCarthy. Men've died for less," Joe warned.

"Well, you are a son of a bitch. You ruined my little girl, damn you. You hanged George for raping that Harvey kid, but what he done is no different from what you did to my Fiona."

"Dammit, man, I never—"

"Shut your mouth, you son of a bitch," Brendan snapped.

Joe's impulse was to take half a step forward and kick McCarthy right in the mouth. Bust his damn face and he wouldn't talk like that.

But Joe did nothing. He stood mute and motionless and took that and all the rest of the invective that Brendan McCarthy poured out onto him. McCarthy was Fiona's pap and that was all there was to it. Joe could not lay a hand on the man no matter what he said. Not without losing Fiona, he couldn't.

The girl—God alone knew why—loved her father, damn him. Joe knew Fiona plenty well enough to know that. And if he had the least lick of sense, Joe Moss had best keep his opinions to himself when it came to Brendan McCarthy, at least when Fiona was around or was apt to find out about it.

No, sir, there was nothing Brendan could say and damn little he could do that he could not get away with. Whether Joe liked it or not.

"Don't be pushin' me," Joe said when Brendan's stream of cussing slowed enough to let him get a word in edgewise. "I love your daughter, and I want—"

"Didn't I tell you to shut your stinking mouth, Moss? Didn't I already tell you that? Don't you know by now that I don't give a fat rat's ass what you want? What I want is for you to keep your filthy hands off my little girl. I can't put her cherry back now you done busted it, but I can damn sure tell you to stay the hell away from her from now on. Stay away. Far away. You don't touch her. You don't talk to her. Do you see her coming, you turn and walk the other way. You hear me? D'you hear me?"

By the time he got all that out he was shouting. Others were plenty close enough to hear and they were for damn sure listening, men and women and probably little kids too.

"You stay away from my little girl, or I'll . . . I'll . . . I'll get you, Moss. I will."

That part was no more than bravado, Joe figured. Brendan McCarthy was not capable of causing physical harm to Joe. But, oh, if the man turned Fiona against Joe, it would be worse than any physical pain could ever be. It would rip Joe's heart clean out of his chest and turn it to dust.

McCarthy was on his feet by then. He screamed a few more curses, then spun around and stalked away past a score or more of stunned onlookers.

Damn McCarthy, Joe thought. And damn that bastard Tarleton too.

Joe's chest was heaving. His blood was up, and if any one of those pissant emigrants had come up to him and said anything right then, it would have been the last thing the poor son of a bitch would ever say for Joe would have welcomed an excuse to use the knife that was still in his hand.

None of them came near, though, or let out a peep. They tiptoed very silently on their way.

Joe stood there for a moment until he could regain control of himself, then turned back to the task at hand. Instead of patiently untying Jonas Farge's rope, however, so it could be returned intact, Joe reached up and made one sharp, quick cut just above the knot, dumping George Tarleton's body unceremoniously to the ground. The corpse fell with a thump and lay there with the noose still in place.

Another slash freed the other end of the rope from the tree where it had been tied off. Joe shoved the bowie back into its sheath and began coiling the now rather nicely stretched rope so he could take it back to Jonas.

✛ 24 ✛

THE TRAIN SLOGGED onward, its progress maddeningly slow as far as Joe was concerned. He had not spoken with Fiona nor so much as stood beside her since that bastard father of hers interfered. Worse, he had not been able to hold her in his arms since that time either.

At night, lying alone under the stars, Joe ached for the feel of her. For the touch of her hair. Her lips. He longed to feel her mouth upon him or her legs wrapped tight around his waist, their bodies joined into one.

And more and more, he was discovering that he missed much more of Fiona than just her body. If he had to, he could get along without that, if only he could touch her and whisper his thoughts and his dreams to her in the night. He loved talking with her, wanted to hear her opinions and to share her desires. He wanted to know what she wanted so that he could give those things to her, whatever they were.

Being apart from Fiona was his notion of Hell. It was driving Joe half crazy.

But there was nothing he could do about it that would not shame her. And so he ached and suffered and yearned to be with her. He lay lonely and alone—the two being two very different sides of a common coin—and thought about Fiona as he drifted in and out of fitful sleep.

What he needed, he figured, was a good blowout. When they got to Fort Laramie, dammit, he would have one. Get knee-walking, bile-puking, dirty-ass drunk. Hire every blanket Indian squaw at the fort and fuck until his balls emptied out and shriveled up. If he was lucky, find some sonuvabitch dumb enough to fight him. A sensible man wouldn't tangle with Joe Moss when he was in a humor this black. But maybe there would be somebody at the fort whose blood Joe could spill. That might make him feel better.

Except, damn it, it would not and he knew it. It was not a fight he needed and not some dusky maiden in his bed.

What he needed, damn it, was Fiona McCarthy. She was the only cure for this disease. And he could not have her. Damn that Brendan anyway for Joe could not have the one woman he'd loved.

She was so close. So close. He could smell the sweet scent of her flesh. Could as good as feel the touch of her. He . . .

Joe came out of his half sleep with a start.

"Shhh," she whispered softly in his ear, so close that he could feel her breath on his skin.

"Is it . . ."

"Shhh," Fiona repeated.

"But your father . . . the people in the train . . . what will they think?"

"I don't care what they think," she whispered. Her lips brushed Joe's eyelids, dipped gently to his mouth, descended to his chest. Her hand was busy inside his trousers. "I don't care. I love you," she said. "Being away from you . . . I couldn't stand it any longer, dear. I love you so much."

Joe groaned. And shot a stream of hot semen into Fiona's hand. "Oh, damn," he mumbled. "It's been s' damn long."

Fiona laughed. "Don't worry, dear. I think I know where we can find some more." She began unbuttoning his britches, exposing him to the chill of the night air. "Let me clean you up first. Then we'll put that where it belongs."

"Oh, darlin' girl, darlin' girl. What're you doing here?"

She half-sat up and laughed again. "You can't figure that out, Joseph?"

"You know what I mean. What about your father?"

"He is sleeping."

"What if he wakes up?"

Fiona's laughter was music to him. "Oh, I don't think he will."

"You got him drunk?"

She shook her head and giggled. "He said he had a pain. So I gave him a spoonful of laudanum. A *big* spoonful. He won't wake up until morning."

"What about the others? What about the folks?"

Fiona turned serious. She practically hissed, "The hell with those people. Why should I care what they think? I care about you, not them. I want to be with you. I need to be with you, Joseph. I love you."

"Oh, darlin', you don't know how I been needing and wantin' you." Joe pulled her down beside him and kissed her, one hand busy with the many tiny buttons on her dress as he did so. He wanted her naked. He wanted to feel the smooth, soft, sweet flesh of her body against his. He wanted the scent of her in his nostrils and the feel of her surrounding and engulfing and accepting him into herself.

"Oh, darlin'," he repeated over and over again as they lay twined tight together in the moonlight.

When they got to Fort Laramie, Joe thought, he would buy some stuff for her. Beads and ribbons and a hand mirror. Silly stuff really, but he wanted to give it to her. Wanted to give it as a token, a sign to signify that he wanted Fiona McCarthy for his wife.

Fiona would not understand that. Not right off. He would explain it to her later. And the other emigrants in the train didn't have to know it at all.

But he'd made up his mind on the subject. When this train got to the Californias, Joseph Moss fully intended to take Fiona McCarthy to wife.

They would live there. Joe did not know what he would do to support her, but the California valleys were fat land. The saying was that if you dropped a seed on the ground, you had to step lively to keep from being poked in the butt by the plant springing out of the earth.

Cattle thrived there too, and horses. He could learn. Crops or cattle either one, he could learn. He hadn't known anything about trapping or trading when he first came to the mountains. He'd made his mistakes, but he'd learned from making them and hadn't made the same ones twice. He expected he could do as much when it came to the raising of crops or livestock.

And Lord knows there was opportunity out there. Most everyone was mad for gold, and gold miners have to eat, have to have clothes to wear and tools to work with.

With Joe's knowledge of trading, it could be he would take up storekeeping once he got to the Californias. He would be paid three hundred dollars in hard money once the train reached the green valleys. He could invest that in shop goods and use the gray as a packhorse to carry his goods around to the gold camps. A man ought to be able to turn a fine profit by doing that.

He and Fiona would marry. He would take up some land—he knew a spot or two that would do more than nicely—and build a sturdy cabin for her. She could put curtains at the windows and those doily things on the arms of the chairs he would make for her. They would put cushions on the chair bottoms and sleep on a mattress stuffed with sweet clover.

Oh, it was going to be fine.

Now that he'd come to the decision, he was plenty excited about it. It was all he could do during those last few nights to keep from telling her all about it.

But not yet. He did not want to say anything about it to Fiona until they got to Fort Laramie and he could buy those foodangles for her. He laughed softly to himself. He had to make it an official sort of engagement after all.

"What are you smiling about?" Fiona whispered.

"I thought you was asleep."

She shook her head. "I'm awake. Just lying here enjoying the air. And being close to you."

Joe opened his mouth. He was sorely tempted. But no. Not yet. The fort was only two days away now. Late the day after tomorrow the way he figured it, they should be there.

He would lead them in and tell them where to set up; then he would be free to slip away and go do his shopping.

For Fiona. For the future. *Their* future.

At that moment, Joe Moss was a very happy man.

✛ 25 ✛

THE HORSES CAME in a rush out of the night, the thunder of their hoofbeats loud. Dark shapes loomed up in the darkness, and an earsplitting shriek preceded the horses.

Joe was already on his feet, tomahawk in hand.

A ball of fire blossomed, throwing bright light into his eyes. He heard the crack of the rifle, but not the sizzle of a passing bullet. He did not know where the shot flew, but it was not close.

Another rifle barked, and he could see that this one was aimed toward the sky. The yipping, yammering warriors wanted to terrify and to confuse.

They must have seen Joe, his flesh pale in the moonlight, for the horses veered toward him.

He crouched, and at the last moment darted to the side. The horses raced past, five, or perhaps as many as eight of them. Their riders were bent low over the necks of the straining animals.

Joe reached out and slapped the shin of the nearest warrior as the man swept by. Having counted coup on the Indian, Joe tipped his head back and let out a whoop to let them know he was aware of the insult he had given, damn them.

Bunch of wild youngsters, he figured, out to raise hell. Probably hoped to steal some horses. Speaking of which . . .

Joe's horses probably would have been swept along with the Indian ponies if they hadn't been hobbled. As it was, they were agitated, but still close by.

"Joseph? Joe?" Fiona's voice was very small and very frightened.

"Right here, darlin'. It's all right. They're gone."

"Help me, Joe. I'm . . . I'm hurt."

Joe's heart felt like it froze in his chest. "Fiona!"

He ran to her, tripped over his bedroll, and went sprawling on top of her. "What . . . oh, God! What happened? Where are you hurt?"

"I . . . I tried to get up. One of those . . . one of the horses ran into me. I think I'm bleeding."

He took her into his arms. "Where, honey? Where 're you hurt?"

"My face. My arm. I don't know."

"Here, baby. Let me see."

There was a split over her left eyebrow. The blood was black as pitch in the night. He could see that the wound was bleeding copiously, but it was more messy than serious. Joe grabbed the first piece of cloth he could reach and held it tight against the split in her fair skin. The cloth happened to be Fiona's dress. He pressed it tight and held it there. If he only had some spiderweb he could use that to stanch the wound. When they got to Fort Laramie perhaps. Except by then the wound would be long since clotted and starting to heal.

"Can you hold this where it is, darlin'? I want to check you for . . . oh, shit. Your arm. No, don't try an' move it. It's broke. I'm pretty sure it's broke. I'll have t' bind it for you. We'll need . . . just a minute." He raised up on his knees and shouted. "Here. Over here. Bring that light."

Someone, a dozen or more someones, with rifles and shotguns, were scurrying about with lanterns. Making perfect targets of themselves if those young would-be warriors were still around, of course, but the emigrants obviously hadn't thought about that.

"I need that light over here," Joe yelled.

The lanterns bobbed closer and a group of panting, anxious men from the train quickly surrounded them.

It was only then that it occurred to Joe that both he and Fiona were bare-ass naked. Years of living among Indians had removed his concern with such things, and it was only now that it was too late that he realized how humiliating this would be for Fiona.

"Well, shit," he mumbled as he grabbed up his blankets and wrapped them around Fiona's trembling shoulders.

But in for a penny, in for a pound. "Hold that light closer. I need to see how bad she's hurt. That's better. Thanks."

As he'd hoped, the split was not a really bad one. She had received a blow to the head and shoulder when one of the horses bumped into her. The contact was almost certainly an accident. The warrior must not have seen her there so low to the ground. Perhaps he was even trying to swerve aside to stay out of Joe's reach. The wound would have to be cleaned and wrapped and it would probably leave a small scar, but it was not serious.

In addition to that, one of the bones in her lower arm was broken. It would need to be set and a splint put on, but that too should heal without long-term consequence.

All in all, he thought, it was not so very bad. Embarrassing. But no more than that.

"Thanks. I'll, uh, I'll walk her back to the wagons an' get her tended to."

Joe stood and unself-consciously found his trousers and pulled them on, then stepped into his moccasins and pulled his shirt on.

"Over here," a voice called from out on the prairie. "I found . . . bring the light. Oh, God! Bring the light." There was a note in that distant voice that Joe did not like. Not at all.

"You," he said, grabbing one of the men by the arm. "Take Miss McCarthy back to your wagon. Get your wife t' take care of her."

"What about—"

"Just do it, dammit." Joe grabbed up his rifle and hurried in the direction of that panicky voice.

"It's the Kramer boy," the voice called. "He's . . . oh, sweet Jesus, he's dead. I think he's been scalped."

Joe broke into a run.

Not that there was any reason to do so. Not now. The wild ones were long gone now.

Tommy was . . . had been . . . one of the youngsters who were watching over the livestock, keeping them herded together overnight.

The band of Indians must have come upon him by accident. Perhaps he confronted them. Tried to fight them even.

Damn it, those warriors had no interest in oxen. Oxen were useless to them except as meat, and they would not take the time to butcher this close to the wagons.

But . . . oh, Lordy.

Samuel Kramer's boy was sprawled on his back, his arms thrown wide and eyes staring sightless toward the stars. His scalp had been lifted and the side of his head bashed in. By a war club, a rifle butt, it did not matter how.

Poor Sam, Joe thought.

Then the others all arrived with the lanterns and Joe's life turned to shit.

✣ 26 ✣

EVERY PERSON IN the train attended the burying of Thomas Andrew Kramer. Every one except for Fiona McCarthy. She was kept away. In shame, Joe thought, after being found naked at Joe's camp. He supposed he could not blame her for wanting to remain in seclusion until some of the gossip and the clucking died down.

That would all end after he got these people to the Californias, though. Joe swore that to himself. He had taken on the job of getting them there, but after that his life would be his own again. And he intended to spend that life with Fiona.

That was one good thing, and something he intended to remind her of the next time he could sneak a chance to talk with her: This sort of scandal became a scandal no more once a marriage was performed. Then it became not a sin, but merely jumping the gun a little.

Fiona needed to keep that in mind for the several months it would take to reach the Californias. Then Joe could come to her openly and claim her for his own.

"Moss!"

"Yes, Samuel?" The burial was over and the emigrants were going back to their wagons to make the last easy pull into Fort Laramie, where they could lay over, resupply, and make sure their oxen and their wagon wheels were in top shape for the harsh desert country that was yet to come. These people had completed the easy part of the journey. The worst was still in the future.

"The board wants to have a word with you."

"Now?"

"Yes. Right now."

Joe did not much care for the expressions on the faces that closed in around him. Kramer naturally looked grim, having just lost his only son to an Indian depredation. But Howard Craddock, James Fenn, Ronald Benson . . . even Martin Lewis looked like his face was carved out of granite this morning.

"What is the problem?" Joe asked.

"You are the problem, sir."

"Come again?"

"You assured us the Indians were friendly."

"The ones I saw an' spoke with were friendly. They didn't bother us none. I don't know who it was that run into your boy last night, but it wouldn't have been any of them that we saw before. Prob'ly it was a raiding party that come upon Tommy by simple bad luck. When we get t' Fort Laramie I'll ask around. See if any group o' young bucks was there lately, maybe liquoring up a little. That woulda made them proddy. Might could account for them killing your boy. Like I said, I'll ask. Not that it'll bring Tommy back even if I do find out, but it might ease you some t' know."

"Fine words, Moss, but the fact is that it was your responsibility to protect us from those savages. You said you could talk to them. You said you could keep us safe from them. Instead of doing that, you were fornicating with a young and impressionable girl, a member of this company. You were derelict in your duty to protect her innocence just as you were derelict, sir, in your duty to protect my son."

"Dere . . . bullshit," Joe snapped. "I signed on to guide this train, not to be your nursemaid. And I have talked to every Indian we seen along the way an' there's been no trouble with any of them. As for those last night, that happened in the middle o' the night when I couldn't of known they were around. If I had known, maybe I could've talked to them, maybe I couldn't. Get a bunch of Indians out for blood and sometimes the only way you can answer them is with blood. I've had to lift enough hair to know that, Samuel. It takes two t' make peace but only one to force a fight. I never gave you no guarantees about anything like that. I done my best every step o' the way here, an' I won't have you saying I was derelict in none of it."

"You conveniently neglect to mention your dalliance with Miss McCarthy. You certainly were derelict in your duties there."

"Samuel, you are starting to piss me off. My feelings for Miss McCarthy are none o' your damn business. Her and me, that's got nothing to do with this emigrant company, and I will thank you to leave her out of any talk."

"There need be no more talk, Moss. About anything. The board has already discussed your situation. We voted . . . unanimously, I might add . . . we voted to terminate your employment. I am sure we can find a suitable replacement at Fort Laramie. If not, we shall simply go on without the assistance of a guide. God knows the road is easy enough to follow. I really do not see why we thought we needed a guide to begin with."

"I'm fired? Just like that?"

"Yes. Just like that, Mr. Moss. We . . . I reluctantly agreed to allow you half the pay you were promised since we are, I am told, roughly halfway to California." Kramer reached into a side pocket and drew out a small pouch. "This will square our account with you."

Joe took the coins from the son of a bitch. There was no point in throwing them back at him. And he had damned well earned this pay, even if Kramer and the other officers of the board did not seem to realize it. They'd had an easy passage thus far not because they did not need Joe, but because he had been doing his job well.

"I've set your pack and a quantity of provisions out for you. You may come by to collect them as soon as you break camp. From that moment on, however, I think it would be best, Moss, if you do not enter this train again."

"What about . . . ?" Shit! What about Fiona? He had to see her. Had to tell her that he would be waiting for her when she got to the Californias.

"There was something more?" Kramer asked. The man's chin came up and there was a flash of defiance in his eyes.

"No. No, I reckon not," Joe said. "You and me are quits. I got nothing more to say t' you."

He strode back to his camp and quickly rolled his bed and took the hobbles off his two horses. The gray he could use to carry his things. That was no problem.

As for seeing Fiona, Joe did not give a fat crap what Samuel Kramer or any of them wanted. He would talk with her and be damned to those others.

He took his little two-horse procession into the wagon encampment and found Kramer's rig in its usual spot at the front. Kramer was busy putting his hitch together. He ignored Joe, which was fine as it relieved Joe of the need to ignore Samuel.

Joe's things were placed in a pile beside the near wheel of Kramer's trailer. He dismounted and spent a few minutes building a pack on the gray, then again swung onto the paint.

He knew—Lord, how very well he knew—where the McCarthy wagon was. He always knew how to find Fiona.

McCarthy's oxen were already yoked up and standing ready to go, but there was no sign of Fiona, not on the seat nor the lazyboard nor standing beside the rig. Joe rode around to the back.

"You ain't welcome here." Fiona was not in sight behind the closed flap, but Brendan was. He had a shotgun in his hands. "Git."

"McCarthy, if you wasn't Fiona's pap, I'd take that gun away from you an' ram it up your ass. Now put it down. You don't need it t' defend yourself. I ain't gonna hurt you. For her sake, I ain't."

Fiona's father continued to hold the shotgun, but he did tip the barrel down so it was no longer aimed directly at Joe.

"I want to see your daughter," he declared.

"You can't. She don't want to see you, Moss, not ever again. You caused her enough grief. Go away. Leave her be."

"I want to take her with me. I want her to come away with me right here an' now."

"She won't go with you. She can't. I need her."

"I don't care what you need, you miserable old son of a bitch. I want to take Fiona to wife."

"Well, you ain't going to, Moss. You ain't never going to. You know why? She made her dying mama a deathbed promise that she'd stick with me, and a deathbed promise can't be broke. She's staying with me, Moss. Now you get your ass outa here. You done enough harm to this family already."

"I won't take your word for that, McCarthy. Fiona loves me. She told me so. She'll come with me. I know she will."

The canvas flap moved and then was pulled aside. Fiona sat there, her beautiful hair disheveled and her complexion red and mottled from hours spent crying.

"Fiona. Darlin'. I come to take—"

"No!" she cut him off. "No, Joseph, I . . . I cannot. Thank you for wanting me. Thank you for showing me what love is. But Papa is right. I made that promise. I promised Mama that I would take care of him. I . . . have to keep my word, Joseph. I will love you for the rest of my life. I swear to you that I shall. But I cannot go with you, Joseph. Not now. Not ever.

"So please . . . don't torment me. Don't make me see you and not be able to be with you. Leave me, Joseph. Please give me that kindness. Leave me. Forget about me. I . . . I wish things were otherwise. But . . . my place is here."

"Darlin', I . . ."

Fiona withdrew and the flap dropped back in place. Closed off his love, his hope, his future.

"Fiona!"

There was no response. Joe sat there, anguished and heartsick. After a moment, he heard Kramer call for the train to roll. Brendan McCarthy walked around to his near leader and prodded his yoke into motion.

Joe was still sitting there on the paint when the last wagon in line rolled past on the clear trail to Fort Laramie.

✣ 27 ✣

JOE'S HEAD WAS pounding and he felt sick to his stomach. The smell coming off his clothes suggested this was not the first time he'd wanted to puke. It took him three tries before he could stagger to his feet. His head was spinning and he wanted to sleep.

The hell with it. He lay back down—more allowed himself to fall than deliberately lay down really—and tried to pass out or sleep or . . . it did not work. He could not escape from consciousness this time. He lay there a while longer, reeking of vomit and urine and the manure he'd been lying in, and finally he gave up and stood again, wobbly but upright.

"Well, shit, look what's alive," old Sol Pennington said when Joe managed to find the front of the building he'd been lying behind and make it inside. "You're a real disappointment to some of the youngsters around here. They been making bets on how long it would be before you drank yourself to death. Or did you just come in to buy another jug? If you did, I might lay some money down on you myself."

"I want . . . I want"—he swallowed back an impulse to void an already empty stomach, the taste in his mouth vile from the gases that seeped out of his throat—"coffee."

"You don't want coffee. I got something better. But I'm not going to waste it on you if all you're going to do is get drunk again."

"I . . . had enough. You know?"

"I should think you've had enough, Joe. Even some of us old-timers from the good old days thought you'd taken it too far this time. I have your things, by the way, your rifle and stuff. I locked them away in my storehouse so they wouldn't get stole by the first light-fingered buck that walked by. Or the greasiest squaw you laid up with."

"Have I . . . how long, Sol?"

Pennington shrugged. "I didn't keep track to the day, mind you, but you've been this way for three, maybe four weeks."

"The K-Kramer train?"

The man nodded. "I remember them. It has been about that long since they passed through."

Joe shuddered. He remembered—vaguely, as if through a fog—thinking to follow the train. Something about protecting Fiona from all the terrible things that could happen between here and the Californias. He remembered—sort of—arriving at Fort Laramie. And he remembered thinking to buy a jug of Injun whiskey to mute the pain he was feeling. None of that worked out quite the way he intended.

"Did they . . . who'd they get to take them the rest of the way, Sol?"

"Crazy Henry."

"He knows the country," Joe agreed. "He's a good man. He'll get them through."

"Of course he will."

Crazy Henry—Henri Dubois—like Sol, like Joe himself, was another of the mountain men from the fur-trapping days. And there was nothing crazy about him. Far from it. He saved himself from a band of Snake Indians once by feigning insanity. The Snakes thought him touched by the spirits; they could not harm someone like that without bringing retribution onto their entire clan, perhaps the whole tribe. Henry was safe enough as long as his captors thought him truly mad. He kept up the pretense, acting the part of a madman for an entire winter, before he got away.

Joe smiled a little, remembering that when Dubois left that bunch of Snakes, he stole back his pack of furs and their whole horse herd as payback for his troubles. Dubois had been known as Crazy Henry ever since. He was a good choice to act as a guide. He would get them through just fine.

But, oh, how it hurt to think . . .

Joe shook his head. The sudden motion almost made him sick. He belched, the taste of it foul, and had the thought that a drink—just one this time—would cut some of the fur off his tongue and take that taste away.

"Here you go, Joe."

Sol Pennington was standing directly in front of him. Joe hadn't noticed Sol come out from behind his store counter. Come to think of it, when did Sol have time to brew the herb tea he was holding out for Joe to drink? He must have missed a few minutes there. Or more than a few.

"Drink this. It will settle your stomach."

Mint, Joe thought. It smelled like wild mint. And maybe something else. Not that it mattered. If the stuff killed him, well, that would be all right too. He didn't have anything to live for anyway, not with Fiona gone from him he didn't.

Sol's tea was steaming hot. Joe burned his lip with the

first sip, and had to wait a moment before he could drink any of it. But it did help to ease the rumbling and the tumbling in his gut.

"That . . . that's good, Sol. Thanks."

"More?"

Joe nodded. Sol took the cup and left. He was back in an eye blink. At least as far as Joe's perceptions had it. It had to have taken longer, but Joe was not aware of that passage of time. He drank a little more of the tea. It did nothing for his head, but the improvement in his stomach was more than welcome.

"Did I make a fool o' myself?"

Sol shrugged and grinned. "Not so much that your friends would care. Who cares about any of the rest of them, no?"

"Thanks. You say you have my gear?"

"Yes, but I don't think you're ready for it yet. You shouldn't try to travel until you are, um, back to feeling yourself, Joe."

"That wasn't what I meant. I was wondering . . . did I leave any money with you? I don't seem to have any."

"Hell, Joe, you were cleaned out by the first fat little squaw you went with. You paid her father to buy her as a permanent wife, but that only lasted until you got drunk enough that you never noticed her leaving. She stayed right here until her band pulled out. Took along everything you had on you, which was everything I hadn't grabbed away from her and put by for you. I think you made her mad, Joe. Her name was Quail Whistling in Morning, but you kept calling her Fiona. I don't think she liked that."

"Jesus," Joe mumbled.

"You called the rest of them that too."

"There were others?"

"Yes. Some."

"How did I . . . I mean, if this Quail girl took my money . . . ?"

"Quail Whistling wasn't a bad-looking girl. You kind of went downhill from there. Some of them I wouldn't piss on, much less dip it into. They were the sort that will lay down and open wide for a swallow or two of whiskey."

"How'd I get all the liquor, Sol?"

Pennington shrugged. "Whiskey is cheap. You have friends, Joe."

"In other words, I begged it off you, Sol."

The storekeeper shrugged again. "You don't have to beg, Joe. Not from me. I owe you, remember?"

"I seem t' remember owing you more than once too, old friend."

"Do you want some advice from an old friend, Joe?"

Joe hesitated for a moment, then said, "Sol, I think I know what you want t' say. But I . . . I don't wanta hear it. You know what I mean? I just don't want t' hear it, never mind that it would be the sensible thing."

"Fair enough," Sol agreed. "We'll say no more about it."

Joe figured Sol was going to tell him to forget about Fiona. It was good advice. And Joe would take it. He would indeed forget about her. On the day he died. Not a minute sooner.

"Could you stand something to eat?" Sol asked.

"No, I don't think so." Joe's stomach clenched and he began to salivate at the mere thought of food. God knows when he last ate. "Could I change my mind about that, Sol? Maybe I could stand a bite after all."

"Good. I'm beginning to think you may live after all." Sol turned and motioned for Joe to come with him into the back of the store where a stew pot was simmering over coals in the big fireplace there. The aroma coming out of the pot was mouthwatering.

Joe was beginning to agree with Sol. He was very likely to live. He was not entirely sure that this was a good thing, however.

A few bites was all Joe could manage before his stomach rebelled against the unexpected intrusion. He wanted to puke again, but was able to keep those few mouthfuls, at least for the moment. Seconds later, he experienced the other effect of prolonged hunger; the food raced through his bowels. Joe had to drop everything and make a desperate run to the outhouse.

When he returned, he walked on rubber legs and his hands were shaking. Sol looked at him and pushed the bowl of stew in front of him again. "Have some more. Just a little. This time it oughta take. While you're eating, I'll get one o' my Injuns to pour some hot water for you. You need a bath, Joe." Sol grinned. "Truth is, Joe, you stink like a sonuvabitch. You stay like that, you'll be driving my customers away."

"Sol, your customers don't have any choice. There's not another store like this'un until they get to the other side o' the Divide. And that's hundreds of miles from here."

The grin returned. "Yeah, an' even so they'd rather wait than smell your sorry ass. Kinda tells you something, don't it."

"All right, dammit. Get that bath ready."

"Fresh clothes too, I think. Those have to be burned."

"Not my shirt, Sol. You can't hardly find doeskin like this. Not made up, you can't."

"That one goes in the fire, Joe. It's flannel for now, old son. You can have a proper leather shirt made up sometime."

"I got to find a job, Sol. Got to pay for all this."

Sol paused, then grunted. "I tell you what. I know of something. Mighty hard work but it'd be good for you. It'll sweat the likker out of your bones. Or kill you. One or t'other."

Joe took a mouthful of the stew and lifted an eyebrow while he chewed.

"Fella I know has a contract from the Army to build some bridges on the road north."

"Shit, I didn't know there was a road to the north."

"There is now. They're building some new posts on the Bozeman Trail. Lots o' traffic moving up that way nowadays. Anyway, this fella I know needs men to drop trees and skid them down to the road and do whatever the hell somebody does to build a bridge. He figures to work right through the winter. Says it'll be easier bringing the timbers down when there's snow on the ground."

Sol dug a finger into his beard and scratched. "Like I said, Joe, it'd be hard work and lots of sweat. Just what you need. Are you interested?"

He did not need time to think about it. "I'm interested, Sol. Yeah, dammit, I'm interested."

"In that case, I'll tell him I found somebody for him. I'll lie like hell and say this Joe Moss fella, he's a good man."

Joe laughed. He hadn't thought he would ever laugh again. But he did.

Friends. What would a man do without them? "Does this mean I got credit with you, Sol? If it does, I'd sure like to buy me a pipe an' a little t'bacco."

"Finish your supper, then you can come pick out whatever you need. We'll get you back on your feet again, Joe. Count on it."

+ **28** +

FOUR AND A half months later, in the middle of a hard-blowing April blizzard, Joe again walked into Sol Pennington's Fort Laramie trading post. He was wrapped to the eyeballs in a robe made of marten furs and was white with ice and snow from the tips of his fur-lined moccasins to the top of his wolf-skin cap.

Four and a half months of hard physical labor had made him sober and lean and damn well tired of swinging an ax or pulling a saw.

"Is that you under all that white stuff, Joe Moss?"

"It's nobody else, Mr. Pennington."

"You best step over by the stove and thaw out some. D'you want a drink?"

"Does a bear shit in the woods?"

"Stand over there, Joe. Andrew, Mr. Gordy, both o' you step aside a little and make room, if you please. I'll make you a mug of something hot, Joe."

"Don't you be giving me no wine now, Sol. I want a man's drink."

Sol hesitated for a moment.

"It's all right, Sol. I don't intend going on no bender."

"You didn't *intend* to the last time as I recall it."

"Yeah, but I had a good reason then." The truth, of course, was that he still had that reason. His heart still felt empty—and colder than the weather outside—because of Fiona. He really did not want to think about her. He could not help himself.

Joe turned to a handsomely dressed gentleman who was among the patrons crowded close to Sol's stove. "You're Hawthorne."

"That's right," the gent said with a nod. "And I remember you. I hired you to work in one of my wood-cutting camps. The job is not done up there surely. Why did you leave?"

"I quit, that's why." Sol brought a tin cup to him, and Joe plunged his nose into it. The toddy was a mixture of whiskey, hot water, and sugar. Joe took a deep, satisfying swallow and smiled. "Ahhh! Now that's what I been wanting."

"Why did you quit, Mr. Moss?" Hawthorne persisted.

"Had kinda a disagreement with the foreman."

"You were on Hansen's crew, were you not?"

"That's right, I was working for Hansen, that square-headed son of a bitch."

Arvid Hansen was a big man, tall and heavily built. He claimed to be the best logger ever to come out of Michigan, and had the skills that might well have allowed him to prove it had there ever been a contest about such things.

"You did not like Hansen?"

"Nope. Not a little bit." Joe finished off the first toddy

and walked to Sol's counter for a refill. When he came back, he opened his coat to allow the heat to reach his body, then took a smaller drink from the freshened mug. "I'll take my pay now," he said to Hawthorne.

"I hired you until the job is done."

"The job is done. For me anyhow." Joe gave Hawthorne a long, unwavering look that sent a chill into the man.

"I suppose I could pay you now, although I might not have enough cash in my pocket at the moment. I was not expecting this, you know."

"You got ten dollars hard money on you?"

"Yes, I should think so."

"Give me that. I'll take the rest in store credit with Sol. Hell, I owe him anyway, prob'ly more than you'll be owing me."

"I can do that," Hawthorne said. He pulled out a leather purse and found two half eagles that he gave to Joe. "There. We should be square now."

Joe nodded. "One more thing," he said.

"Yes?"

"Your man Hansen?"

"Yes."

"He's dead."

"He . . . what happened?"

Joe took another drink. "Damn, this is good." He wiped his mouth and said, "I killed him."

"Jesus Christ!"

"He thought because he was foreman he owned me an' the Indian woman I had up there too. Thought he could just walk into my lodge and have some of that. The funny thing is, if he'd been a decent sort an' just asked, I might've loaned her to him. But he thought because he was the boss an' because he was big, he could just take what he wanted. So I killed him."

"You . . ."

"That's right. I did. I thought you oughta know, your wood-cutting camp bein' without a foreman and all."

"You're joking with me. Aren't you?"

Joe finished his drink. "Am I laughing?"

"What . . . what will happen now?"

"The other boys have Hansen laid out in the harness shed. Cold as it is, I expect he'll keep until the ground thaws out and they can bury him. Unless you want t' send a wagon and bury him down here. He's your man. It's up to you."

"But . . . the law. What about the law? How will . . . ?"

"Mr. Hawthorne, the law ends somewhere back around St. Jo. Not that there's any need for it when it comes to Hansen. All I done was to take care of what was mine. A man's got a right to that."

Hawthorne looked like he might be sick to his stomach.

"Don't fret yourself," Joe told him. "Hansen ain't much of a loss. There's a young fella up there . . . Lester Tice his name is . . . who can run that crew for you better than Hansen ever did. He knows the boys an' they respect him. They'll work for him. Do you put him in charge, you won't be disappointed."

"I don't understand," Hawthorne said.

" 'Bout what?"

"You. You mur . . . you killed my foreman. Now you're being helpful, even recommending his replacement. That is what I do not comprehend."

"Hell, Mr. Hawthorne, I ain't mad at you. You didn't do nothing to hurt me. Why should I blame you for what Hansen done?"

Hawthorne shook his head. He looked confused.

"You'll have t' excuse me now," Joe told him. "I haven't

eat in a couple, three days an' my nose tells me Sol has something on the cook stove in the back."

"Yes, uh . . . well, all right."

Joe touched the front of his shaggy fur cap, shrugged out of the marten robe, and strode away, following Sol into the back.

Sol chuckled. "You shocked that poor man, Joe."

Moss grinned at his old friend. "Reckon I did at that."

"Hansen was a big one."

"So's a bear, but I've killed enough o' them in my time. D'you still have my rifle an' stuff put away somewhere, Sol?"

"Yes, of course."

"Then I expect I'll wait out this storm an' light out."

"Are you going back East to pick up another wagon train?"

"Not no way. I'm quits with the Oregon Trail and the Californias, Sol. I won't be taking that route again." Not knowing where they had gone or what had happened to them, he did not want to risk running into Fiona or her father at the western end of the road if he should guide another train there. "No, what I think I'll do is head down to where it's warm. Taos or Santa Fe, someplace like that. Maybe pick up some work freighting. Lots of traffic on the Santa Fe Trail these days, or so I'm told."

"There's a lot of unrest back East," Sol said. "Some say there will be a war back there. There's a lot of hard feelings about tariffs and slavery and like that."

Joe shrugged. "That don't mean nothing to me. I don't care what those folks back East want t' do just so they leave me alone. That's all I want, Sol, is to be left the hell alone."

"If you say so."

"I do."

"Then I wish you luck, my friend." Sol smiled. "But you already knew that. Now shut up and let me get you something to eat. No more liquor, though. Not until you have some food in your belly. Then maybe you and me can have ourselves one last drunk before you go."

✢ 29 ✢

JOE CAME IN out of the blowing wind. He stopped just inside the arched doorway to brush some of the snow off his poncho and to shake the mane of hair that fell to his shoulders. He needed a haircut and that was a fact. A haircut and bath first, he was thinking, then a drink and a woman, all of those among the reasons he was always glad to return to Santa Fe. "You wanted to see me, Lemuel?"

The owner of the freighting company nodded and stood, coming around from behind his desk to shake Joe's hand and guide him to a chair. "You got through all right? No losses?"

Joe removed his wide-brimmed straw hat and dropped it onto the floor beside his chair. He thought about stripping the woolen poncho off as well, but decided not to bother with that despite the heat since he expected to be here for only a few minutes. Lemuel Higgins kept a fire blazing in the beehive fireplace, and the office felt overly warm. But then Joe had not set foot inside a building of any sort in well over a month; his body was acclimated to being out of doors. "We lost one mule to a broke leg, but that was the only loss."

"That's what I like about you, Moss," Higgins said. "You're reliable. I can count on you to get my trains through."

Joe shrugged his shoulders. He hoped Lemuel would not keep him long. He was tired.

Higgins returned to his swivel chair and steepled his fingers, staring into his hands in deep thought. Finally he looked up. "Reliable. That's you."

"Something in your mind, Lemuel?"

"You and I, Joe, we've never talked about politics."

"I don't know anything about politics, Lemuel. Don't give a shit about any o' that either." The conflict that Sol Pennington first mentioned to him two, three years ago had become a reality. Back East—hell, on this side of the Mississippi too—the country had split north against south. Armies were fighting great battles. Or so everyone said. Joe paid little attention to fights he was not involved in, and he himself had no dog in this fight. He neither knew nor cared anything about tariffs, and as for the slavery thing, he had no strong feelings either way. He had never owned another human being nor wanted to, but there had always been slaves. Civilized whites owned Negroes. Indian tribes owned other Indians . . . and a good many whites too. Joe's experience was that the slaves who truly wanted freedom found a way to gain it . . . and then often acquired slaves of their own.

"I trust you, Joe," Higgins said, leaning forward and lowering his voice. "Can you keep a confidence?"

"If you want me to, sure."

"I have . . . Joe, I want you to do a special job for me.

Well, for someone else really. But I would consider it a favor. A personal favor."

"Name it then, Lemuel. But you know I ain't gonna promise you anything till I know what it is you're talking about here."

Higgins glanced toward the closed door and reduced his voice again almost to a whisper. "There is little money involved and there would be great risk. I want you to understand that right up front, Joe."

"Fine, but what the hell 're you asking for here?"

Lemuel leaned closer. "The South, Joe. The Confederate States of America."

"What 've they got t' do with anything?"

"The Confederacy needs gold, Joe. The country needs money to purchase arms and foods in order to resist the invaders."

"I wouldn't know anything about that, Lemuel."

"Joe, the Confederacy needs gold, and the West is the great producer of gold. Colorado, California, Nevada . . . Joe, the Confederacy needs the West, needs the production of those mines."

"All right, but I ain't got nothing to do with that."

"Oh, but you do, Joe. If the Confederacy can send an army to take New Mexico and Colorado, we can split the West off from the Union. We can control the output from those mining districts. Maybe from California too. This is important, Joe. It is critically important. That is why I want you to do your part for the cause of the South. I want you to join our forces in Texas. I want you to guide our Army into New Mexico and help us face the enemy. Right here in Santa Fe. We need to capture Santa Fe, Joe. You can help us do that. And then after we control Santa Fe—"

"Whoa!"

"What?"

"You're talkin' to the wrong fella here, Lemuel. I told you. I got no interest in politics. I appreciate the offer of the job, but I ain't your man. Not for this."

Higgins's expression turned hard. "I thought I could rely on you, Moss."

"An' so you can, Lemuel. If I take a job on, I'll see it through. But this job, Lemuel, I ain't taking on."

"May I remind you that you gave me your word you would hold this conversation in confidence?"

"I'm not gonna tell anybody about this, Lemuel. I'm not gonna go running to the Union Army if that's what you are thinking. I got no more interest in their side than in yours."

"Yes, well, um . . . very well. We will just leave it at that," Higgins said stiffly. "I misjudged you. I apologize."

"No need for that, Lemuel. No need at all to apologize for you ain't done nothing that needs apologizin' for."

"I, uh, I will have your pay ready for you this afternoon if that is all right."

"Whatever you want, Lemuel. You always been straight with me an' I trust you to do what's right."

"Fine. Come back this afternoon then. Late this afternoon."

Joe shrugged. It was not the way Lemuel normally did business. Usually, he paid off on the spot. But the man would have his reasons. Whatever those reasons were, Joe trusted Lemuel Higgins. The delay would give him time to go get that bath and haircut. The woman and the drink could wait until Lemuel paid him for this latest trip back to Missouri and the return to Santa Fe.

Joe picked up his hat and stood.

"Check with me later, Joe. I'll see that you are taken care of."

"I know that, Lemuel."

"Do you mind if I ask you something?"

"Anything you like." Joe grinned. "I'll either tell you the honest truth or a real believable lie."

Higgins laughed. "I'm just curious about something. I don't believe I've ever seen you before without that toma-hawk you generally carry."

Joe touched the front of the poncho he'd acquired before he pulled out of Santa Fe this last trip east. "Got it right here, Lemuel. Reckon I wouldn't feel comfortable with it close t' hand."

"And those old horse pistols? Do you still have those?"

"No, I got rid of those when I was in St. Louie."

"Fine. I was, uh, just curious. I hope I didn't offend you."

"O' course not, Lemuel. If you'll excuse me then, I wanta get cleaned up. The look on the faces of people standing downwind from me makes me think I need one."

Higgins laughed again. "I will see you later then, Joe."

Joe touched the brim of his hat and left the heat in the office. For a few moments, the cold wind outside felt almost good. It picked up the hem of his poncho and swept underneath, lifting it briefly to expose the Colt's revolving pistol Joe had traded his old single-shot horse pistols in on with that St. Louis gunsmith.

That war back East had accomplished one thing that Joe Moss found to be worthwhile; it had advanced weapons technology by leaps and bounds. In this one Colt pistol he had five shots, while there were only two in the pair of old guns. Even more amazing, there was now a rifle with self-contained ammunition. A Henry repeating rifle that used brass-cased cartridges and held fourteen of them at a time. Joe had already replaced his old muzzle-loading mountain rifle with a Henry.

But the tomahawk and the bowie . . . he expected he would have those with him right up until the day he died.

He tilted his hat to block some of the wind that was seeping down the back of his neck and set out for the nearest barbershop so he could get that haircut and bath.

✢ 30 ✢

Damn, it felt good to be clean again. He emerged from the casa where he kept a room—ground floor on the courtyard so he could slip an overnight visitor in if he felt like it without anyone the wiser—wearing clean drawers, clean britches, even a clean hunting shirt. Joe was walking tall and feeling good. And he would feel even better when he had that pay in his pocket.

That would be the last, though, he thought, from Lemuel Higgins. He had nothing against agents of the Confederate States, not any more than he had against agents of the United States. But he did not want to get caught up in their politics. He did not really give a crap who wanted to write laws and make fancy proclamations back East, and he certainly was not going to take sides about something that held no interest for him.

So everything considered, it probably would be best for him and Lemuel to go their separate ways. God knows Joe could work for any freighter in the Santa Fe. They all knew him. They all knew they could count on him. Many of them had made offers to him in the past, but Joe had remained loyal to the man who'd helped him break in down here. Now it was time for him to pull his stakes, he figured.

As he walked through the gathering evening on his way to Lemuel's office, he was thinking over the possibilities. Whoever he went with, it would have to be one of the mule-whackers. Oxen were too damn slow and horses too tender. A man could count on mules. A grin flickered across Joe's freshly shaved features. If he could cope with their stubbornness, that is. Joe had come to really enjoy working with mules these past few years. They—

Fire bloomed, a huge orange ball of it, out of an alley mouth to his left, and a pistol ball plucked at the heavy wool of his poncho.

A second shot, much louder, and the fireball much larger than the first, followed from Joe's right. He felt a hard punch in his chest and belly. A shotgun.

Jesus! He'd been shot straight on with a shotgun.

He staggered but was still upright, still on his feet and able to move, although he did not see how.

He clawed the revolving pistol out from under the poncho and returned the fire of the one with the shotgun.

Joe heard a grunt and a curse and the sound of a falling body.

The man in the alley shot again, and this time the ball found its mark. He felt the impact high on his chest.

First hit with the shotgun. Now with a pistol ball. Joe figured he was a dead man. Had to be. He was bleeding and growing weak.

But he wasn't dead yet, and if he went then, those sons of bitches were going down with him.

He stepped with deliberate care lest he lose his precarious balance and go down before he was ready.

Walked to the mouth of the alley.

A man, someone Joe never saw before in his life, stood there frantically trying to reload one of a brace of pistols.

Joe cocked his Colt's pistol and put a .44-caliber ball into the man's chest.

He swayed, felt himself growing weak. He pulled the trigger of the revolver again. Damn gun was empty. Funny, he did not remember firing that many times.

Not that it mattered.

There was not very much that mattered.

Except that he was getting very tired.

Losing blood. He knew the feeling. It was one he had felt before.

But not like this. Not when he was shot point-blank, first with a shotgun and then with a pistol.

He was dying. The bastards had killed him.

It happened. Everyone dies.

Joc pushed the revolver back into his sash and took hold of the old tomahawk that had stood him in such good stead for so many years.

It would serve him still.

The man in the alley was down. On his knees. Staring up in horror as Joe's tomahawk descended.

Then a dark shadow fell over Joe's eyes. That was the last thing he saw. The last he knew.

✠ 31 ✠

CONSCIOUSNESS RETURNED SLOWLY, and with it came pain. Joe had known pain before, and he welcomed it. The pain meant that he lived. He was pleased with that. And pleased as well to know that those who'd tried to kill him did not live. Most of them. There was at least one who survived. He was sure of that. The one who sent those others was still alive.

Joe's eyelids fluttered. For one awful moment, he thought he was somehow blinded. Then he realized that the problem was only that it was night. Of course. He remembered now. It was been close to dark when he was attacked. He could clearly remember how bright the muzzle flashes from their guns had been. Could remember them as clearly as if he was still seeing them. Pistol flare on his left. Much bigger and brighter shotgun burst to his right.

They'd been waiting for him all right. For him in particular. He was sure of it. And sure too that he knew why.

Lemuel Higgins had exposed himself as an agent of the

South who was working against the interests of the Union garrison here at Santa Fe. He'd told Joe about his plans, and when Joe rejected Lemuel's overtures, he'd preferred to have Joe killed rather than accept Joe's promise of silence. The fool! Joe was a man who would stand by his word. No matter the provocation, if he once gave his word, he would honor it.

Well, he would continue to honor his word this time as well.

But if he continued to live, he would have a different sort of word with Lemuel Higgins. That too Joe swore as he lay in . . .

Where? Come to think of it, just where the hell *was* he?

He was no longer lying in the street or in that alley where he'd killed that one with the pistols. He was pretty sure of that. He could not see, but he could feel. A little. And aside from the pain that lay deep in his chest, he was fairly sure that he was lying on something soft.

Blankets? Someone's bed? Had someone found him and carried him back to his room?

Not his own room, he thought. Where he lay did not feel like his own bed. And this place did not smell like his room either. This place smelled of woman. And chili peppers. Charcoal and fried tortillas. Incense. Or possibly a perfume of some sort.

A Mexican woman then. One of the many he'd taken to bed since he came here? He could not think of any among those who would go out of their way for him. Those had all been commercial encounters, bought and paid for and with no involvement of the heart. Joe had had quite enough pain of the heart with Fiona McCarthy. He did not want to experience that again. Not ever.

No, surely none of those happy little whores would drag him in off the street to bind his wounds and put him to bed.

Then who?

He closed his eyes to think about the question.

The next thing he knew, there was bright daylight showing around the edges of a Navajo blanket suspended over the window in a room he had never seen before.

Joe turned his head, even that small movement sending a bolt of pain shooting through him. He winced, and immediately a soft voice spoke in his ear. "You are awake."

Joe tried to speak but could not. His lips, his tongue, his throat were parched, the lips glued tight shut with dried mucus and saliva. All he got out was a groan.

A moment more and he saw a shadow above his face, felt the cool touch of a damp cloth. He heard the sound of trickling water. It took him a second or two to figure out that whoever spoke—it was a woman's voice—whoever spoke to him was wringing out a cloth in a basin of cool water.

The cloth laved his forehead. His eyes. Passed across his mouth and onto his neck. Nothing had ever felt so welcome, so very good.

He tried again, and this time managed to open his mouth and pry his eyes completely open. "Who . . . where . . . ?"

A face moved into range of his vision.

An angel? Did angels come to earth and tend to the weary or the wounded?

The woman was young. In her twenties perhaps or early thirties. She was Mexican, but this was no bar girl. She was . . . elegant. Beautiful really, despite the worry that furrowed her forehead and pursed her lips. Very full lips, Joe noticed. They appeared soft. And red.

She had luminous brown eyes and a black mantilla over long black hair that shimmered with health.

Her gown was expensive, the sort of thing a wealthy American woman might wear. Joe knew nothing about ladies' clothing, but he was sure about that. This was no common woman.

So what the hell was he doing here? This room surely was in her home. He had no idea, however, who she was or where.

"Who?" he asked again, the single syllable coming out as a croak barely recognizable as human speech. "Wha . . . ?"

The woman smiled. "My name is Isabelle de la Cruz. *Mrs.* de la Cruz. You are in my home. I found you on the street. I thought you were dying. I had you brought here so you would not die alone in the dirt." She laughed, the sound of it warm and soft. "You fooled me, sir. You did not die. Not that I am complaining about that, you understand."

She had only the faintest accent, he noticed. This woman had been speaking English as well as Spanish for much of her life.

"When?"

"How long have you been here, do you mean?"

He managed a very slight nod.

"You have been here a little more than two weeks."

Joe's surprise must have showed. She added, "The doctor says you should not have survived at all. He says you must have a truly remarkable constitution and an even stronger will to live. You were very badly wounded. If you had not been wearing that poncho, he tells me, you would have died for sure. The blanket absorbed much of the force of the shotgun pellets. He picked a great many out of you."

A great many pellets, Joe thought. That meant the asshole with the shotgun had used small shot in his load. If he had been using buckshot, probably Joe would have been killed by that first charge. Joe hoped he'd killed the bastard.

"Others," he said after taking a moment to swallow. "The men . . . shot me . . . did they . . . are they dead?"

"They?" Mrs. de la Cruz said.

"Two. Two men. Shot me."

"I do not know anything about that, sir. You were alone in the street when I found you. There was no one else close by. I had you picked up in my carriage. We brought you here." She smiled. "It pleases me that you did not die. Of course."

"Gracias," he said.

Mrs. de la Cruz laughed again. He liked the sound of it. "It is very kind of you to try out a word of Spanish, but it is not necessary. And your accent is really quite"—her laughter filled the room—"quite terrible."

Joe smiled. Or thought he did. Tried to.

He felt the touch of her damp cloth.

Heard a soft buzz that might have been her voice but coming from some distant place.

And then he was gone again.

✛ 32 ✛

DESPITE LIVING IN—or at least working out of—Santa Fe for the past several years, Joe had little contact with the local Mexicans. Other than the bar girls, that is, and he had to be fairly drunk before any of them interested him. Drunk enough to believe that they looked like Fiona McCarthy to him, and that was quite drunk indeed.

As a consequence, he was apprehensive about being in the care now of Isabelle de la Cruz, and all the more so about being treated by a Mexican physician.

Dr. German Guttierez was short and plump and uninspiring to look at. He was also, however, gentle and thorough and knowledgeable. He prescribed few medications, but much time on a padded settee that the house servants moved into the courtyard. Even in winter, the strong sunlight was warm and pleasant with the courtyard walls blocking the chill cut of the wind.

Joe was fed broth by the gallon, so much that he feared for the chicken population of Santa Fe and its environs, and an odd, musty-tasting tea that Guttierez insisted he drink. Joe did not know what the tea was made of and did not particularly want to know. Whatever it was, he was sure he had consumed worse in the past. And it did seem to help strengthen him.

The household quickly enough fell into a routine that included Joe and his needs. In the morning, he would be given tea and a light breakfast. Later, when the sun was well up, his chair would be carried into the courtyard and windbreaks would be placed close by if there was a breeze. He would take his lunch in the sunshine, and there was tea ready to hand.

Tea going in meant tea coming out, of course, and Joe was too weak to walk. He could not get up and go to the water closet, or even find some privacy to use a thunder mug. That problem was solved with a lap robe and tall, narrow jar.

The first time Mrs. de la Cruz took it from him to empty and clean, he was embarrassed. Hell, he wasn't sure highborn women like her ever had to take a leak. Well, maybe they did. But he did not want to know about it.

Several weeks into his convalescence, he was still much too weak to get up and walk without assistance. The physical weakness was hard for him to accept. All his life he had been robust. Strong and healthy and ready for anything, even when he had wounds to heal from. This wound was somehow different. His breath came shallow and his muscles would not cooperate. His wounds seemed to be healing, yet he felt a deep heaviness in his chest that was unlike anything he ever experienced before.

Isabelle de la Cruz and the doctor came to him one sunny afternoon. They pulled chairs close to his chair and sat beside him.

"There is a . . . how you say this, eh?" Guttierez had little

English and Joe even less in the way of Spanish. The doctor went into consultation with Isabelle, who translated the doctor's words into English.

"There is a ball. A small one from the shotgun, not the ball from the pistol. You know this difference?"

Joe nodded. "Yeah, I do." A double-aught buckshot was the same size as the ball from a .36-caliber pistol. The shooter who attacked Joe had obviously chosen a lighter shot size in his gun that evening, something suitable for small game perhaps or waterfowl.

"One of these reached your lung, Mr. Moss. It is still there. You will not fully heal unless it is removed."

"Surgery, you mean?" Joe spoke to Isabelle but his eyes were on Guttierez. The little man's appearance did nothing to inspire confidence. "Like with a knife and everything?"

"Yes, Mr. Moss. Like with a knife. And everything."

"Jesus!"

"Please do not use that name except in prayer, Mr. Moss."

"Oh. Sorry. But this gent . . . he wants to cut my chest open?"

The lady and the doctor spoke at some length in language Joe could not begin to fathom. Finally, Isabelle turned to Joe and said, "He would cut as little as possible. If he is fortunate, a probe will find the ball and be able to"—she had to think for a moment to find the word she wanted—"extract this thing that is in you."

"And if I don't let him do this?"

Isabella and Guttierez conferred again, then she said, "You have this right. The choice must be yours. If you remain as you are, know that you will heal. The flesh will pull together. Your chest and your lung will show no outward signs of distress. But your strength will never again be as it was. You will be short of breath. No, um, stamina. That is it.

You will lack stamina. But nothing more than that. You will be able to live a perfectly normal life even though that ball remains within you."

The doctor said something and Isabelle added, "He wants me to explain that there is no immediate need to decide. A week more, even two if you need this time to make up your mind. Pray about this, Mr. Moss. Pray for guidance and for wisdom."

"What about if he does do it? Is he sure I'll be all right after that?"

"There is not a certainty, Mr. Moss. The surgery might do no good at all. Or you could die from it. That is possible. It is not likely, but he wants you to know that it is possible." Isabelle touched Joe's wrist. "He is a very good doctor, Mr. Moss. And this I tell you, not he."

Joe closed his eyes and rolled his head to the side so that he was facing away from these two who were so kind to him. After a moment, he heard them whisper and then they stood and moved quietly away so that he could be alone to think.

Pray, she'd said. Joe was not much of a praying man. Never had been, and he wasn't going to run bawling and whining now that he was bad hurt.

But he did think.

Fiona was what he thought about. Fiona and the future he had wanted to build with her. A home, a real one, and a family.

Without Fiona, there would never be either of those. He knew that. If he had Guttierez's surgery, he could die, she'd said. Hell, he didn't really care all that much about dying. Everybody does it, one time or another. And without Fiona, there wasn't much point in living anyway.

Without her, life had no flavor to it. No substance or depth or color.

No, he was not frightened of death. But to live weak and short of breath, half-invalid for the rest of his life?

It wasn't all that much of a worry then, was it. Not when he got right down to thinking about it.

The hell with it. Let the pudgy doctor do whatever he damn pleased.

Joe figured he would tell them that just as soon as he woke up from his afternoon nap.

✠ 33 ✠

THE SURGERY WAS not so bad. Or maybe it was. Joe could not really remember.

They brought him tequila. *Lots* of tequila. That part of it was certainly pleasant enough. While he was still aware of what they were doing, while he was still drinking the tequila, they lifted him onto the big butcher-block table in the kitchen of Mrs. de la Cruz's hacienda and strapped him down with heavy harness leathers.

He remembered people, more than just Dr. Guttierez, moving around the table. Talking. He could hear them clearly, although later he could never remember anything that was said, only that he had heard the voices at the time.

He remembered pain. Not so much that he remembered the actual feel of the pain, but he remembered the fact of it. He knew there had been sharp, biting pain that drove deep inside his body.

And he remembered that there was one last, stabbing

lance of pain. After that he passed out and remembered nothing more.

When he woke up, he was told he had been unconscious for more than twenty-four hours.

"Did he . . . did the doctor get the ball out?"

Isabelle smiled. "But of course. Do you want to keep it for a souvenir? He saved it for you if you would like to have it."

"No, I . . . thank you but no."

"Then I shall return it to German. He is quite proud of himself for the extraction. I think he would like to have it."

"He's more than welcome to it. Will he come by today? I need to thank him. And . . . I need to thank you too. You've . . . I would've died without all you've done for me. I know that. What I don't know, if you don't mind me askin', is why you've done all this for me. I'm nothing to a lady like you, just some stranger lying half-dead in the street one night. You could've drove on by and nobody would've faulted you for that. Instead, you brought me into your home. You've taken care of me. Fed me. Even arranged that surgery. I don't hardly know how to thank you proper."

The lady smiled. "I am a Christian woman, Mr. Moss. When I saw you, I saw you not as a man but as an opportunity to serve my God. I hope that does not offend you, to be used like that. So impersonally. I must say that knowing you now, I am pleased that things have turned out so well. You seem a good man, Mr. Moss. You have a new life. I hope you will live it well."

She paused. "Have I said something wrong? Something to hurt you?"

"No, of course not."

"Your expression tells me otherwise, Mr. Moss. Do you not wish to live a good life now?"

"The truth . . . it isn't something I like to talk about but . . . reckon I owe you more than I've ever owed anybody in my whole life. I won't try an' hide anything from you. It's just . . . any hope I had for a good life was ruined years ago."

"This that you speak of, it would have something to do with the girl you call Fiona?"

"Fi . . . how d'you know that name?"

"You were very vocal when German was preparing you for the operation. The alcohol loosened your tongue, Mr. Moss. Your only thoughts seemed to be of this Fiona." Isabelle pulled her chair a little closer and leaned forward to take Joe's hand in both of hers. "Tell me about her, Mr. Moss. Tell me about this Fiona of yours."

He did. Reluctantly but honestly. And almost completely. There were a few details that he omitted, but those were left out to protect Fiona's reputation, not his own.

"You love her very much," Isabelle said when he was done.

"I did."

"Not 'did,' Mr. Moss. 'Do.' You still do."

"Yeah, I . . . I suppose maybe I do."

"Will you try to find her again now that you have a fresh new life to live?"

"No. Never," Joe said. "She made it clear that we was quits. She made that promise to her mama. She wasn't lying about that nor making excuses. I was there. I heard her at the time. I just didn't . . . didn't realize her promise would take her away from me and mess up my life too. I won't try and see her again. It wouldn't be fair to her and . . . I don't know as I could stand it neither, seeing her but not bein' able to, well, you know."

"Yes, I do know, Mr. Moss. I lost my husband just about the same time that you say you lost your one true love. I know that pain. My husband is dead but I still miss him. Every day. All the time." She sighed. "At least you have the satisfaction of knowing that your Fiona is alive and well somewhere in California."

Joe turned his head away. Isabelle was wrong there, he thought. She was a widow who still loved and missed her husband, but at least she knew that he was gone forever. That was cut and dried; there was no possibility of turning back from it. Joe, however, had no sense of ending. For him, all was uncertainty. He did not know where Fiona was. Or how she was. Or even if she was still alive.

No, he thought, Isabelle had the better situation, knowing she was a widow, able to put her life back together if she were able to do so, while Joe remained anguished and uncertain, never knowing what had happened to Fiona after the Kramer train rolled on west and left him at Fort Laramie.

He felt an odd sensation of heat behind his eyes, felt Isabelle wipe them with a soft cloth.

"I am sorry," she said. "I did not intend to bring bad memories back to you. Forgive me, please."

"Nothin' to forgive, ma'am. Really."

"Yes, of course." She gave his hand a squeeze and stood, her skirts rustling. "Go to sleep, Mr. Moss. German will be here this afternoon to see to your progress."

Joe did not answer. He lay silent, trying to let go and escape into sleep. Healing sleep.

But perhaps, he thought before he dropped off, perhaps it would have been better if Isabelle de la Cruz hadn't driven past the alley that night. It might have been much better if she had just allowed him to lie there and die in the street.

✠ 34 ✠

IT WAS ANOTHER six weeks before Joe shaved and dressed and, for the first time since he entered Mrs. de la Cruz's house, appeared on the veranda with his tomahawk and bowie knife in his sash. They had been recovered with him that night, but his Colt's revolving pistol was missing, presumably taken by whoever it was that picked up and spirited away the bodies of the two men who'd tried to kill Joe.

"You are . . . you are leaving us, Mr. Moss?" Isabelle seemed surprised. She set her cup aside and rose to face him.

Joe took a half step back. "Yeah, I . . . it's time. I need t' go." He was not quite completely healed after the shooting and the surgery afterward. But it was time for him to go. It really was.

"Is something wrong, Mr. Moss?"

"No. Of course not. Nothing." But in fact there was. He needed to leave. Had to. And had to do it now or perhaps . . .

The truth, a truth he could not come right out and put

into words, was that he was a man. And it had been a long time since he had been with a woman.

Isabella de la Cruz was a woman. And it had been a long time since her husband's death.

There was . . . something . . . between them. Something unspoken but growing. And Joe was afraid if he did not leave this house now, he would take this good woman into his arms. He was afraid that anything of that nature would shatter Isabelle's innate decency and goodness. It would shame her. Worse, it would shame Fiona and the love Joe still felt for her.

No, he had to leave and he had to do it now while he still could.

"I think . . ." She paused, and he thought perhaps she lightly sighed and squared her shoulders in acceptance of all that lay unsaid but was more and more powerfully felt. "Will you come back to see us?"

"Yes," he lied. "I'd like that."

She nodded. "Good then. What can I do for you to help you on your way? Do you need money? Anything?"

"Nothing, thanks. I have some money. That wasn't stole from me." He supposed Isabelle was assuming that he had been waylaid by a thief that night. He had never explained the truth to her.

"All right then." The silence between them was awkward.

"I want t' thank you. I don't know . . . I know better'n to try and pay you. There's no money can be enough to pay for what all you done for me, and you didn't do what you done because you wanted paid for it. I know that. But I . . . I want to thank you and I don't know how. Nothing I can think of would be enough."

Isabelle smiled. She stepped closer to him and raised onto tiptoes to brush Joe's cheek with her own. He felt the warmth of her, and the scent of her filled his nostrils. His body immediately reacted, and like a boy in his teens at his first dance, Joe desperately hoped Isabelle would not notice the telltale bulge in his trousers.

"You owe me nothing. You allowed me to serve my God as if I were a Samaritan and you the pious man."

Joe did not know what she was talking about. But he did know Isabelle was far off the mark if she was thinking he was some sort of pious fellow. "I reckon, well, I expect I'd best be going now."

"All right. Yes."

"Isabelle? Miz de la Cruz?"

"Yes?"

"Thank you. That's the only way I know to say it. Thank you. For everything."

The lady smiled. "The pleasure has been mine, Mr. Moss. And please do drop by again now and then when you find yourself in our fair city. I would like to keep abreast of your travels. I would like to know if you ever see your Fiona again."

"I'll do that." He would not. She probably understood that quite as well as Joe did. "I'll be sure an' do it. And please give Dr. Guttierez my regards an' my thanks too. I owe him almost as much as I owe you."

"Yes, well . . ." She thrust her hand forward, and he took it lightly into his fingers. Her flesh was warm and he felt something pass between them at that small contact. Isabelle quickly pulled her hand away.

"Well . . . good-bye then, Miz de la Cruz."

"Good-bye, Mr. Moss."

Joe turned and strode at something just short of a run to the front gate. He let himself out and hurried down the street, having to look around frequently until he got his bearings and discovered just where he was. He had been unconscious the night he was brought here, and had not been outside the walls of the de la Cruz hacienda since that night.

It was a good four miles to the house where Joe roomed, and he was not as fully recovered as he'd thought. He was winded by the time he reached home and let himself in.

A good sleep would take care of most of what ailed him, he thought. A good sleep, a few drinks, perhaps a woman. He should be up to that now. As long as they didn't get too rambunctious.

For now, though, he wanted to rest up a bit and change his clothes. He let himself into his room.

And stopped short, staring.

What the hell was this?

Joe's things were gone. His clothing. His trunk. His Henry repeating rifle. His saddle and gear. Everything that had been familiar to him was gone now and someone else's things hung from the wall pegs. Someone else's razor and hairbrush were laid out on the small table. Someone else's boots were lined up beneath the bed.

Joe spun around and went storming off to find the elderly lady who owned the house.

"But Mr. Moss," she squeaked when he found her in her kitchen. "I was told you were dead."

"Well, I ain't dead, dammit, and you had no right to give my room to somebody else."

"I am sorry. I truly am. But what can I do?" She spread her hands in a show of innocence. "I thought you were dead."

"Where's all my stuff?"

"I sold it."

"All of it?"

"Everything except that funny-looking rifle gun. Emory liked that. I said he could keep it." Emory was the lady's son. He was older than Joe, but was soft in the head and would be a child for all his life.

"You gave Emory a gun, ma'am? How could you do a thing like that? Who knows who he could hurt now that he has a gun."

"Oh, I didn't give him the bullets, Mr. Moss. I just let him have the gun in his room like a, well, like a toy you might say."

"What I do say is that I want my rifle. And the bullets. An' I want whatever money you collected when you sold the stuff you stole from me."

"I didn't . . ."

"Yeah, yeah, you thought I was dead. Fine. But I want the rest o' my stuff, ma'am. Most of all, I want that rifle and the cartridges for it."

"I will get them for you right away, Mr. Moss. Wait here. I'll be right back."

I T WAS EVENING by the time Joe reached the office of Higgins Freight Company. That was fine. Lemuel would likely still be there. Counting his damn money, Joe thought.

He let himself in without knocking, the Henry rifle in his hand. Lemuel was behind his desk, just as Joe expected he would be. It had been months since Joe had been inside this room, but nothing had changed except possibly the papers on the big desk where Higgins sat.

It was springtime now, but the huge, mule-drawn freight wagons would still be rolling, Santa Fe to St. Louis and return the whole year around, and this man reaping the profit with each and every trip. This man and his Confederate pals. Joe did not care a fig about any of that, not the business part of it nor the politics, and never had. Lemuel Higgins apparently did not, perhaps could not, understand that.

When Joe walked in on him, Higgins looked up. He turned as pale as if he'd seen a ghost. And of course he had.

"Moss, you . . . I thought you were dead."

"I was just taking a vacation, so t' speak."

"But . . ." Higgins took a kerchief from his breast pocket and wiped his forehead and his hands. "It, uh, it is very good to see you, Joe."

"Yeah, I been looking forward to this my own self," Joe told him. He rested the muzzle of the .44-caliber Henry on the front edge of Lemuel's desk. The barrel happened, as if by accident, to be pointing to Lemuel's belly.

"Oh, don't . . ." The man recoiled, shoving his chair back from the desk as if the polished wood had suddenly become red hot.

"Don't what, Lemuel?"

"I thought . . . why are you here, Joe?"

"Why, I come t' collect my pay for that last pull I made for you. I was gonna come back for it that night but I never made it this far. You remember that, Lemuel? Do you?"

"Yes, I . . . of course I do. Yes." Higgins nervously wiped his face and hands again.

"I'd like my money now, Lemuel. If you don't mind."

"Of course. I'll get it for you."

"Now, Lemuel."

"Yes, I have it right here. I, uh, I put it away for you."

"I thought you said it was your understandin' that I was dead, Lemuel. Why'd you go an' put money aside for a dead man?"

"I meant that I still owe you. And I have enough here to pay you. Of course."

"Glad t' see me alive now, are you, Lemuel?"

"Yes. Very happy. Very."

"You all right there, Lemuel? You look awful pale."

"The, uh, the shock. You understand. Thinking you dead. And . . . everything."

"Yeah. I wouldn't wanta forget that 'everything.' "

"Will you . . . will you be wanting to take another train for me, Joe?"

"I reckon not, Lemuel. Not when you consider 'everything.' "

"Yes, well, uh, let me get your money. This will only take a second."

Higgins wiped his face again and stood. He went to a cabinet standing at the wall behind his desk and opened it, then knelt. An iron safe was built into the cabinet. Higgins fumbled in his vest pocket for a key, unlocked the safe, and pulled it open.

"Right here," he said over his shoulder. "I keep some cash here."

"O' course."

"I am sure I have enough to cover your back wages. How much did you say I owe you?"

"I can't remember for certain sure, Lemuel, but I'd think it must be considerable. When you think about 'everything.' "

"Yes. Of course. Everything."

"Lemuel, you don't look real healthy right now. D'you think you oughta set down for a minute?"

"Yes. Thank you." He pulled a lockbox out of the safe, a gray steel container about the size of a loaf of bread, and put it on his desk. "Joe, would you mind moving that . . . that gun? It makes me nervous."

"Sorry. Guess I wasn't thinking." Joe placed the Henry on the desk, the barrel lying atop some of Higgins's papers, and took a step back leaving the rifle there.

"Thank you. Now if I can find the key to this box, I will be happy to give you what I owe you." Higgins opened a drawer on the right side of the desk and reached in.

When his hand came out he was holding a pistol. He cocked it and aimed it at Joe.

"Why, Lemuel, you do surprise me. With my own damn gun? That is my revolver you got there, isn't it?"

"I am sorry, Joe. I like you. I always have. But after I unburdened myself to you and then you rejected the Cause . . . let's just consider this to be a casualty of war."

Joe began backing slowly away from Higgins and the revolver.

"You can't run fast enough to evade a bullet, Joe."

"I ain't running, Lemuel."

"No?"

"No, y'see what I am doin', what I already have done, is get the distance just what it has t' be."

"The distance?" Higgins looked puzzled. "What distance?"

"Why, the distance between you an' me, Lemuel. You got to have the distance right so's the spin works out an' you don't hit something handle-first."

"I don't understand."

And then very likely he did. But too late.

Joe's hand flashed and the tomahawk flew, whirling blade over handle, spinning in the air to make exactly one turn before it buried itself in Lemuel Higgins's chest.

The .44 Colt in Higgins's hand fired as the man reflexively clutched at it when he saw the tomahawk flying toward him. Flame and smoke filled the room for a moment, and the ball from the pistol missed its mark as Joe darted to the side.

Higgins did not have time enough to cock and fire a second time. Before he could hit the floor, Joe leaped over the desk and grabbed Higgins by the throat, slamming him back against the wall with Joe's tomahawk still in his chest.

The man was still alive when Joe pulled his bowie and

took Higgins's scalp, then slashed his throat open with a cut so deep it nearly severed the head from the body.

Joe dropped what was left of Lemuel Higgins and retrieved his tomahawk, wiping both the 'hawk and the bowie on Lemuel's handsomely tailored suit.

He gave Higgins's body a glare and angrily kicked it somewhere in the midsection. Not that Higgins knew or could any longer care.

Joe stepped wide of the pool of bright blood that was spreading over the floor. He shoved the tomahawk and the bowie back into his sash and picked up the revolver, his own revolver, and placed it in his sash beside the bowie, then went to the desk.

Higgins probably had a key to the lockbox somewhere, but Joe was not going to bother searching for it. He took up the steel box and tucked it under his arm. He went around to the front of the desk and with his free hand picked up the Henry rifle.

A door into the clerk's tiny office squeaked open unexpectedly. "Mr. Higgins? I thought I heard . . . my God!"

A thin young man Joe had never seen before stood there gaping at the sight that greeted him in the boss's office. But then it must have seemed a rather grizzly scene to him. Lemuel Higgins's body lay sprawled in a vast pool of fresh, foul-smelling blood.

And there was this armed stranger staring at him from only a few feet away.

The young man took it all in. And fainted dead away.

Joe snorted. But it was a shame, he thought. The young fellow had seen him. Did not know who he was but had certainly seen him, and as far as the authorities would know, this would be a robbery and murder.

It would probably be a good idea, Joe thought, for him to leave Santa Fe now.

Probably a very good idea indeed.

Joe took his things, which now included the steel box and whatever it contained, and left the poor clerk passed out on the office floor close to the remains of his employer.

Yes, sir, Joe's time in Santa Fe was pretty definitely used up now. He needed to move along.

✤ 36 ✤

THE FIRST THING Joe needed was some privacy. He walked across the square in front of the Governor's Palace to one of the cantinas, and went around back to a porch where a lantern hung lighting the way for patrons who needed to use the row of outhouses behind the block of buildings.

Joe took down the lantern and carried it with him into an outhouse, the powerful smell enveloping him when he closed and latched the door behind him. He set Lemuel Higgins's lockbox on the one side of the seat, wedging it into the corner where the front and back walls joined, and placed the lantern on the other side out of the way.

Four sharp jabs with the curved brass butt-plate of the Henry rifle served quite well in place of the key Higgins claimed to have been looking for. Joe prized open the lid and whistled softly. Lemuel kept enough in there to pay what he owed Joe all right. And then some.

Joe did not take time to count the twenty-dollar double

eagles that were in one pouch, or the ten-dollar eagles in another leather drawstring bag, or the hefty contents of a third pouch, but he was sure there had to be hundreds of dollars in coin there. He put all three pouches into his possibles bag and fingered through the stacks of paper money in the box. There were two, the thicker being currency issued by the Confederate States of America, the other United States paper money. Paper currency was little used and poorly accepted anywhere in the Western territories, but a man could sometimes find someone who could be talked into taking it. And, of course, post offices had to accept it. With that in mind, it seemed something of a pity to Joe that he had no one he wanted to mail anything to.

He put the paper U.S. money into his bag along with the gold. The Confederate bills no one in his right mind would take. He dropped those into the foul-smelling effluvium beneath the privy seat.

He riffled quickly through a thin sheaf of documents also contained in the lockbox. Mostly those seemed to be bills of sale for livestock. A deed to the building where the freight company offices were located. Several other papers written in Spanish. Joe had no idea what any of those might have been. They could have been maps pointing the way to Montezuma's lost treasure for all he knew. He shrugged and dropped them all, the broken lockbox included, into the liquid slop below the seat.

And while he was in the neighborhood and had an opportunity, he turned around, dropped his britches, and had a satisfying dump. Then he picked up the rifle, returned the lantern to its place on the cantina's back porch, and went on his way.

He avoided the freight yard, where he was certain to be recognized, and walked to a livery barn that he had passed a hundred times or more but never had reason to do business with, letting himself in and calling out for whoever was in charge.

He was pleased when the voice that responded did so in English. "I'm closed, dammit. Come back tomorrow."

"But I need a horse," Joe said. "Tonight."

"I haven't had my supper yet."

"I haven't had mine yet either, but I still need a horse."

"I don't have any rig available to rent right now. My buggy is busted down and my only wagon is already out being used somewheres."

"I don't want to rent it and it isn't a driving rig that I need. I want to buy me a horse. Or a mule if you have one that's trained to the saddle."

"You don't want a mule," the voice from inside the tack room insisted. "Nobody in his right mind wants a mule."

"Well, I want one. Or a horse. Any damn thing I can ride. And I'll be wanting a saddle for it too."

"Where you going that you can't wait to morning?"

"The Californias," Joe said. "Me and another fellow got a nice little business started there, but I just got word that my partner is down sick. He needs me to help out until he's on his feet again."

"California? That's a long way."

"Yeah, an' that's why I want to get started. I don't want to lose everything we got invested. That's why I need that horse. I need to get south to the stage route. Once I get to El Paso, I can sell the horse and take a coach the rest of the way, but the quicker I get down there the better. I'm in a hurry, mister. But I have money. I can pay."

"What kind o' money? American? Mexican? Paper? What?" the voice inquired, sounding more interested now.

"Hard money," Joe told him. "American. Gold."

The tack room door opened and a bald-headed man peeked out. The fellow was smiling. "Let's you and me do us some business, friend. Let's us get you on your way to California."

They would do some business all right, Joe figured, but like hell he would be going to California. Not ever again did he intend to go there.

And he would not be going to El Paso del Norte either, at least not any time soon. It would not hurt if the law thought he was headed that way, however. By now, there would be a hue and cry on for a man of his description.

Fair enough, Joe thought. Taos was not all that far. He expected if he could just get out of Santa Fe tonight, he could outfit in Taos. Buy a pack animal there along with provisions and some gear. Then he could head up into the San Juans or perhaps on up to the Bayou Salado. He hadn't been in the South Park country for years.

Spring, he thought, should be a fine time of year to travel.

And the faster the better.

"Now show me what you have, neighbor," Joe said to the eager livery man.

✦ 37 ✦

JOE DREW REIN atop the last hill, just as he broke out of a clump of quakies. The whole, vast array of South Park lay before him, green and rolling, a pocket of grass ringed by the white peaks of mountains, whole ranges of which lay here like waves on the sea. But here, here in South Park, there was a prairie, the great, grassy plains displayed in miniature. Twenty, thirty miles or so in any direction and all of it prime. It was one of Joe's favorite places.

Joe drew rein and sat atop the tough little Palouse horse, just taking in the handsome view and breathing deep of the crystal air. Barely visible on the grass below him was a band of pronghorns. In the hills nearby he knew there were countless mule deer and elk, perhaps even a few remaining buffalo, although the last time he was up here it had seemed to him that the buffalo were becoming scarce.

Joe liked South Park. Always had. He'd sometimes thought it was a place where he could stand to settle—if ever he decided to settle—except for the fact there was no way a man could make a living up here. There was not enough of a growing season for a man to farm, not enough beaver for a man to make his way by trapping, not enough people moving through, Indian or white either one, for a man to make it by trading. But he liked this country. He surely did.

He sat there for several minutes, telling himself he was allowing the Palouse horse a blow. But the truth was that Joe was simply enjoying the basin of grass that lay before him. The spotted horse was in no real need of rest despite the climb it had been making ever since they left the Arkansas River behind.

That was one thing about a Palouse. The spotted horses were tough. You couldn't hardly wear them down. They tended to be stupid, though, even as horses go. And horses are among the stupidest of critters to begin with. But the Palouse was plenty tough, at least as tough as the little mule that trailed along at the end of a lead rope, and that was more than good enough for Joe.

He'd picked up both the Palouse and the mule in Taos, swapping off the nag he bought from the livery barn down in Santa Fe, and outfitted in Taos as well.

Now he was thinking he might just put up some sort of rough shelter and stay for the approaching summer. He had some basic supplies and there was enough game in the Bayou Salado to feed a small army, never mind one man. He calculated if he was lucky, he could probably go the next couple months here without seeing another human person, and a little solitude would be a joy.

When he used up what he had with him and had to move along, he could just drop down to the east, emerging from the mountains below Pikes Peak. There were settlements there nowadays where a man could get a drink and whatever else he craved.

But for now . . . Joe grunted softly, the mule's ears pricking forward at the sound, for now it sounded mighty fine to spend time just to himself. It would allow him to get the stink of cities out of his nostrils.

"All right, boys, let's us get along now," Joe murmured aloud. He heeled the Palouse to a walk and pointed it onto a dimly visible game trail that wound through the rocks and scrub oak on this hillside overlooking the south end of South Park.

"Aw, shit!" Joe pulled the Palouse to a halt and stood in his stirrups, the better to see what lay ahead.

There was a road. Right here in South Park. It was a real road too, cut by wagon wheels, and not just a trail scratched out by travois poles dragged behind a Ute pony, the occasional presence of Utes being the price a man had to pay for staying in the basin. But now there was a *road* here. It was enough to make a man think there was no place left where he could get off by himself if he felt like it. A road!

He cussed again and then a little more, and then as he continued past the road, his displeasure was compounded when he realized he could see smoke up ahead. Several thin smoke columns. Like from chimneys.

They were rising in a clump of activity from beside one of the streams that took its head up here, those streams flowing off to the four winds, the ones to the north being the headwaters of the South Platte, the eastern flow contributing to Fountain Creek down on the plains, and those draining south and west making their way down to the Arkansas River.

Now one of those many streams seemed to be feeding a settlement of some sort. Rough cabins, Joe saw as he came closer to them. Crudely constructed out of aspen or pine, some roofed with weathered canvas. But cabins they were.

White men's dwellings. Whatever the hell they were doing up here . . .

Joe could see men wading in the creek now. Or digging in it and feeding gravel into a rocker or a Long Tom.

Gold!

Aw, shit indeed, he thought. If there was gold up here, the solitude of South Park had been breached and would never be the same again.

Joe wondered if any of these intruders had coffee made. He could surely use a cup. Better, he could use a good long drink of something with some kick to it. He damn sure felt like he needed a drink.

"THAT'S FIFTY CENTS, friend."

"Mister, I'm buying a glass of the stuff, not the whole bottle. Hell, truth is it ain't even a full glass. Look there. It's only three-quarters full. An' come to think of it, what for sort of a bottle is that you're pouring out of? This stuff never saw the inside of a bottle till you finished stirring it an' poured it into that one there."

"You don't like it, don't drink it. But if you want to drink it, you pay me my fifty cents or I'll lay a bung starter upside your head."

Joe glared at the man. But paid him the half-dollar. For one short glass of whiskey. A price like that was worse than they used to charge at Rendezvous. It was criminal was what it was, criminal. He took a drink of the whiskey and made a face. That was criminal too. "Mister," he said, "I been in the Indian trade since before you was wearing long pants. I oughta teach you how to make

Injun whiskey that a man can drink. This stuff tastes like buffalo piss."

The barkeep just stared at him.

Joe finished his drink, grinned, and asked for another, reaching into his possibles bag for the other half of that dollar.

"I thought you didn't like my concoction."

"I don't. But it's the only whiskey I know of around here. If there's another place, just tell me where."

The bartender, who seemed also to serve the tiny community as a storekeeper, trader, and perhaps half a dozen other ways as well, poured Joe's second drink. This time he filled the glass to the brim.

"Thanks." Joe raised the glass to him in salute and took another swallow, then smacked his lips. "It's a fine thing, I tell you."

"The whiskey?"

Joe's grin returned. "No. The fact that liquor starts to taste better after that first glass or two no matter how bad it is t' start with. Now that is what I call a fine thing indeed."

The bartender laughed and topped off Joe's glass without asking for payment.

"You don't seem to be doin' much trade here," Joe observed. He was the only customer in the flimsy, low-roofed cabin.

"Enough. Everybody's out working their claims right now. Come nightfall, they'll want to spend whatever they find. Mind if I ask you something?"

"Go ahead."

"You paid with coins, not dust. You come up here to stake a claim of your own? 'Cause I got to tell you all the good pockets are already taken. They been picked over pretty hard."

"No, I'm not a mining man. Never have been. I spent enough time wading in cold-water streams when I was hunting for beaver. I don't wanta do any more of it. I'm just passing through and thought I'd have me a drink, maybe a meal somebody other than me has cooked. You got anything to eat like that?"

"I will have. My woman will be putting something together this afternoon. It'll be ready by the time the fellas put their tools away and come looking for it."

Joe nodded. "Then I expect I'll be back. No point in pushing on at this time o' day when I can get that meal in a few hours."

"You sound like a man who's in no hurry."

"No hurry at all," Joe said. "I haven't decided what to do next. Maybe go up into the Blackfoot country an' do some trading again." It was something he'd been thinking of since shortly after he made his rather hurried departure from Santa Fe. And Lord knows he had enough capital in what he took from Higgins to start off with a good stock of trade goods. The idea of opening another trading post sounded good to him. Especially if it was located far from Santa Fe.

"I'd be a-scared of the Blackfoot," the barkeep observed, leaning his elbows on his own pine-slab bar. "You hear bad things about them."

"Things like what?"

"Like they kill all the white folks they see and scalp them. I never seen a man scalped and I don't want to. Even more, friend, I don't want to be scalped my own self."

"Yet you're here in Ute country," Joe responded.

"Oh, the Utes, they're tame. Some of them speaks English even. We got some hang around here and hire out for day labor digging gravel or whatever. My woman that will be cooking for you tonight, she's Ute. Cheerful, fat little

．

thing. Does whatever I tell her and never a word of complaint. But I sure wouldn't feel so easy around your Blackfoot."

"Now you see, there's the difference in the way we look at things. I've lived among the Blackfoot before an' know they aren't no threat. Not any more. They used t' be known as Bug's Boys, but not no more. An' if one of them gives his word about something he'll keep it, same as a Lakota or a Cheyenne will. Your Utes, on the other hand, they're the lyingest pack of sons of bitches I ever come across. Treacherous too. You know where this bunch learned their English?"

"No, of course not."

"You better hope it wasn't down to Pueblo settlement. Though it very likely could've been."

"Why would that make a difference?"

"Couple years ago . . . four or five maybe . . . a band o' Utes befriended the whole town of Pueblo. Moved right in as helpers. Studied English. Went to school. Went to church even. The folks was real proud of their friendship with those nice Utes. Then come Christmas, they invited the Indians to services with them. Except the whites left their guns at home while Utes showed up with guns and knives and axes. They killed damn near every white in that part of the country. More'n fifty souls if I remember aright." Joe finished the glass of whiskey. "Me, I'll stick with my Blackfeet, thank you."

The barkeep turned pale. "They've . . . one of the men was asking the other day if we had us a church up here yet."

"Might not mean a thing," Joe said. "Could be a different band entirely. But it's hard to know, ain't it." He held his hand over top of the mug when the bartender moved to fill it. "I think I've changed my mind, friend. That's enough firewater for me today. An' I reckon I'll move along and settle for my own cooking until I can get down to Fountain or one of those other new towns down below." He nodded. "Thanks for the whiskey an' the conversation."

He was on his way again within minutes.

✦ 39 ✦

THAT WAS ONE fine plan shot to hell by the march of civilization, Joe thought as he rode down out of the mountains to the rolling plains below. But there were always the Blackfoot. Surely no one would ever want to take up residence in that distant country.

He finally got his other-cooked meal in a café in Fountain, close by the banks of the creek of that name. The place, he was startled to discover, was built mostly of sawn lumber instead of logs or wattle. What the hell was the world coming to if there were sawmills and ladies'-wear stores all the way out here. Amazing!

Joe had had a bellyful of cities, but he did ride into Denver instead of passing it by. He could get the trade goods he wanted from Sol Pennington, and anyway would rather deal with a friend than with some stranger, but this far into the traveling season, good mules would likely be in short supply at Fort Laramie. And the big, wagon-dragging Missouri mules that might be found there after they were worn down by the road and swapped in for something fresher were not exactly the sort of stock he wanted for his pack string. For that he preferred the smaller, lighter, easier-mannered little Spanish mules.

Had he known how this would turn out, he could have bought all the Spanish mules he wanted when he was down in Taos.

Of course, he'd been in something of a hurry when he left that country. In Denver, he was able to take his time and pick over the available animals until he had a string that satisfied him. In the end, he rode out of Denver City with five mules trailing behind the spotted-rump Palouse horse.

He took his time on the trip between the South Platte and the North, letting the mules become accustomed to each other and to him. By the time he bought his trade goods, he calculated, and got up into Blackfoot country, he would still have several months before serious winter. Time enough to establish his trading post and let the word get out that Mankiller was there and open for business.

If he could make a living at the venture, well, that was all he was after. The truth was that he was more interested in solitude than in profit. His days of ambition and excitement were done. They'd rumbled off to the Californias with the Kramer train those years back. Damn it.

Joe still felt the stab of acute loss every time he thought of Fiona, and no amount of whiskey or of women since then had been able to diminish his feelings toward her.

And the worst of it was that he had never once come right out and told her that he loved her.

He did. Surely she knew that he did. But as far as he could recall, he had never actually spoken the words to her.

Which was, when he thought about it, rather bitterly amusing. In the course of a carelessly spent life, Joe Moss had drunkenly pawed a hundred cheap and easy women and told a good half of them that he loved them.

Yet the one good woman who he genuinely did love never heard him say the words.

Thinking about that only made him want to pick a fight and bust some son of a bitch's head open.

He got his chance when he rode into Fort Laramie and tied up outside Sol's store.

✛ 40 ✛

"**W**HAT THE HELL . . . ?"
　　　He heard the scuffle of feet on the hard ground.
Then a few grunts. And then something he was sure of, the
dull and meaty thud of fists striking flesh. Someone was
having a fight.

Joe stepped around the corner of the store building to
take a look. It was not his intention to become involved. It
really wasn't.

But he could see a tall, thin, gray-haired man in leather
skins, surrounded by four burly men who looked like the
freighters and bull-whackers Joe had known and dealt with
while he was working in the Santa Fe trade. Freighters can
be a rough lot. And there were four of them who were pum-
meling one lone victim here.

It hardly seemed fair. All the less so when the gray-haired
old fellow's fur hat came off and Joe got a better look at him.

"Well, I'll be damned. Mind if I take a hand, boys?" Joe
asked, just as politely as he knew how.

He stepped forward and brought a clubbed fist crashing down on the back of the nearest bull-whacker's neck. The fellow's knees wobbled, but he stayed upright. Joe turned him around and hit him again with a hard right to the jaw. That was enough to put his lamp out. His eyes rolled back in his head and he sank to the ground.

"Hey. This is a private fight," one of the 'whackers protested.

"Not no more, it ain't."

"Joseph! *Mon ami*. You want this one too? I can finish these others if you take the one more."

"It's a deal," Joe yelped, his chest filling with the lust of combat and the pad of muscle over the back of his neck and his shoulders swelling like those of a bull elk in rut. He felt . . . good, dammit. Happy. He threw his head back and laughed loud and long.

The reaction seemed to confuse the hell out of the bull-whacker Henri Dubois had just given to Joe as an adversary.

"You can't do this. It ain't right," the bull-whacker protested.

"Then you best stop me from it, friend." Joe stepped in and poked a left into the man's face, landing the blow on the bridge of the fellow's nose. Not at all that hard really, just enough to sting him and get some tears and snot running.

"Dámmit!" the 'whacker bleated.

Joe figured he'd already given the man quite enough chances. And besides, the one he'd already put on the ground was trying to get his feet under him. In a few more seconds there would be the two of them to face, so . . .

Joe busted the 'whacker in the face again, stepped in close, and threw a very hard body blow and landed square in the breadbasket. The man doubled over. Joe stepped back, judged his distance, and kicked. At the first one he'd put down, wanting to keep that one occupied before he got off his knees. The fellow did seem almighty big. He had shoulders like an ox and legs like tree trunks. Joe figured he could play with the other one if he wanted, but the big fella could make this thing serious if he wanted.

Joe's kick landed on the big man's nose. Shaped flesh turned to pulp and blood flew as the big fellow's head snapped back. His eyes rolled white and he was out again.

The other one jumped in while Joe was occupied with the big boy. Joe felt—heard more than felt—the thud of a hard fist landing. His own head snapped back and his face went instantly numb.

Joe blocked a left jab, ducked under a roundhouse right, and leaned in to tattoo his opponent's belly with a series of quick punches before he backed out in time to avoid a knee that would have crushed some particularly cherished bits of his anatomy.

"Now, now," Joe gently chided. And threw a vicious uppercut that would have taken the man's head off had it landed.

Annoyed with himself for missing the uppercut, he followed it with a left cross that landed on the cheekbone and skittered across to push the fellow's nose to the side.

"Dammit!" the bull-whacker yelped. "That hurt."

Joe began to chuckle. "Come morning, friend, you are gonna look like a raccoon. You'll have you some big-ass black eyes."

The bull-whacker laughed, any seriousness of intention gone now. Nearby, Crazy Henry and his pair of freighters were coming to a similar conclusion. Henry's right ear was torn and blood covered his lower face and neck and from the way he was holding himself, kind of hunched over and hurting, it appeared that he had been a mite slow to stop someone's knee.

On the other hand, the two he'd been fighting were battered and bleeding worse than Henry was.

Come to think of it . . .

Joe ran a hand under his nose and peered at it. Sure enough, it came away smeared with crimson from a nosebleed from the one really good one he'd been tagged with.

"You all right?" the bull-whacker asked as he helped his twice-beaten friend to his feet. The big man did not look to be completely in touch with the real world just yet, and his legs were rubbery. He draped an arm over his pal's shoulders for support once he was upright.

"I'm good," Joe said. "You?"

The bull-whacker grinned and felt of his jaw, working it back and forth a little. "Nothing busted."

"Good. You want a drink?"

"Are you boys buying?"

"Hell, yes. Ain't we, Henry?"

"Ain' we what?"

"Buying whiskey."

"You got money, Joe?"

"I got money."

Crazy Henry turned to the four bull-whackers, his pair and Joe's too, and announced, "My friend an' me, we are buying."

The six men crowded inside Sol's store in search of a jug they could share.

Damn but he was glad he'd come back up to this country. It beat hell out of any city Joe ever saw or heard of, it surely did.

IT WAS BARELY dawn. But what exact morning Joe was not sure. He just might have missed one there. Or two.

His head pounded, his stomach rumbled sourly, his tongue tasted so bad he wanted to spit it out. Yeah, he was glad he had come back. There was nothing quite like being among men who understood him.

Joe took Big Frank by the hair and lifted his face off the table. There was no discernible response, so he let the big fellow's head drop. It hit the table with a painful thump. It was probably a good thing that Big Frank could not feel anything.

Anthony was awake, though. He looked at Joe and grinned, turned his head, and spit on the floor.

Floor. They were in Sol's store. Inside. That was important. If Sol hadn't dragged them out back and pitched them into the mud, it hadn't been a bad drunk, just a pleasant one. Joe blinked a little and rubbed his face, trying to get used to the idea of sobering up.

Anthony hefted a half-gallon crockery jug of trade whiskey and offered it to Joe, who shook his head. He'd had enough. He had enjoyed it, but now he had had enough.

Joe levered himself upright, standing on his own hind legs as if for the first time. The wobbly efforts of a newborn foal to rise came to mind. That was exactly what he felt like. He swayed back and forth a little, but did not fall down, which he took as a good sign.

He tried a step. And then another.

No one was behind Sol's counter. That did not matter. Joe needed something to lean on. He gave his weight to it, took a deep breath, and bellowed, "Pennington, you son of a bitch, where are you when I need you?"

"You don't need me," a voice came from the back. "You need coffee. I'm coming with it."

"Well, hurry then."

"You up to having something to eat too?" Sol said as he came into view with a coffeepot and fistful of tin mugs.

"I'm s' hungry, Sol, I wouldn't waste time skinning it did I have a dead beaver."

"Here then. You boys start on the coffee. I'll see what I can scrape up for food."

Joe grinned at him and chuckled.

"Have fun, did you, Joe?"

"Shit, yes. But whyn't you join us?"

"I did. Some. But somebody has to pay attention to business or the movers and the Indians would steal me blind. Now set down at the table again and get some of this into you." Sol put the coffeepot and the mugs down in the middle of the big table where Crazy Henry and the others were beginning to stir in response to the aroma of fresh-boiled coffee. There was nothing, Joe thought, that smelled better than coffee, especially when you were in need of a cup.

Joe sat down in the same chair he'd occupied for however

long they had been here, and helped himself to the coffee. He only spilled a little of it. And, oh, it did taste fine.

"That's better," he whispered reverently.

"Surely is," Bertram agreed a little too loudly. The four bull-whackers were pretty good boys once a fella got to know them. Couldn't fight worth crap, of course. But pretty good boys all in all.

"Gimme some of that, will you?"

The coffee made its way around the table until all of them were awake. More or less.

"How long we been here?"

"I dunno. You?"

Joe shrugged. It wasn't like it mattered.

"I hope that damn swamper's kept our stock watered an' the thieves outa the wagons."

"We better be pushing along."

Joe rubbed his face and reached for more coffee. "Where you boys going?"

"North. They're building them some kinda Army fort up the road a piece. We got goods to deliver there."

"Mind some company along the way? I'll be going north myself quick as I outfit. That won't take but a day or so."

"Yeah, you come with us. We can wait for you."

Crazy Henry smacked his lips and gulped for air. He did not look like he felt very good this morning. "Where you go up there, Joe? Why you go?"

"Gonna do some trading. You wanta come with me? Wanta partner up and see how we make out?"

"Where?"

"Oh, I dunno exactly. I was thinking to go into the Blackfoot country."

"Yah, I could do dat with you, Joe."

"We'll get some geegaws and stuff from Sol. I got a little string o' mules."

"Mules," one of the bull-whacker snorted.

"You got something against mules?"

"Hey, I ain't looking to fight nobody. Mules is fine with me."

"All right then." Joe turned his attention to Crazy Henry, the two of them talking about the things they would want to carry as trade goods. Soon the bull-whackers got up and left the table. Joe pulled his chair around closer to Henry's and reached again for the coffeepot, which was empty. "Sol!"

"I'm coming. Here. Have some porridge. That oughta be easy in your bellies. I'll bring you some more coffee."

" 'Ey, Joe, you mind I ask you something?"

"Ask me anything you want. We're partners now, ain't we."

"Whatever happen wid dat kid of yours, eh? What ever happen wid dat girl you knock up?"

"Kid?" Joe frowned for a moment in thought. 'You mean with that Crow girl I had a while back? I thought you knew. I gave her to Three Rabbits. Last I knew she was all bellied up, but I never knew what kinda kid she had."

"No, no, not dat one. Her I know about. I mean 'at white girl."

"I never knocked up no white girl, Henry."

"Oh, hell, yes. Maybe you don' remember she. Skinny girl. The hair red like a t'ree-point blanket. Pretty ting. In dat train I take over for you 'at time long time ago now. Time you get fire right here. You remember her?"

"Henry, I never—"

"Yah, Joe. She knock up bigger'n melon, belly out to here. Ever'body say 'at Joe Moss, he the daddy."

Joe froze. For the space of a heartbeat, all of time and sight and feeling came to a dead stop. He felt his head spin and his stomach lurch.

Jesus God!

Fiona. She'd been pregnant?

God, what had he *done!*

"Henry, I . . . I . . ."

"You din' know?" Henry shrugged. "You mus' be a daddy long time now, Joe. 'Ey. Joe! Where you go, huh? Joe?"

✤ 42 ✤

To honor the partnership they had agreed to, Joe gave Crazy Henry the spare mules and a hundred dollars toward a stock of trade goods, but the Palouse horse and the tough little mule he'd gotten in Taos he kept for himself.

"Where you go so sudden, Joe?"

"The Californias, friend. Where'd you say you left that train?"

"Sacramento Valley like all of they."

"Then that's where I'm headed. I got to . . . I got to find that girl. Make things right by her."

"Joe, I know you how many years, eh? You never been serious 'bout no female. 'Cept maybe horse, maybe beaver."

Joe only shook his head and stood. He grabbed a bundle of jerked buffalo from Sol, thanked his friends, and hurried away.

Fiona. What had he done to her? Ruined her life probably. Everyone who had been in that train—and everyone

they met in California—would know her for a fallen woman.
A wanton.

Her father was a son of a bitch to begin with. How
would he have acted when his own daughter was the object
of scorn in whatever community they went to? There was
no telling what he might have done.

He could have turned her away. Forced her to become . . . anything. A woman alone. With no husband, no
marketable skills, no hope for the future. Ridiculed. Out-
cast.

God!

It was Joe's fault. All of it. Whatever had happened to
Fiona, whatever ugliness she'd had to endure . . . it was all
because of Joe.

And he'd never even told her, actually told her in so
many words, never really told her that he loved her.

Which he did. Oh, how he did. He had ached for her for
the years since he last saw her. No amount of whiskey, no
number of women had been able to smother that love.

Now . . . only now to learn that he had a son! Or a
daughter. That did not matter. Or . . . oh, God, what if the
baby had died? What if Fiona had died in childbirth?

Women did that, he knew. White women in particular.
That was what he'd heard. White women were fragile any-
way. And Fiona, dear Fiona, was so slender, so slightly built.
How could she have withstood the demands of pregnancy?
The baby might well have died. *Fiona* might well have died!

He did not know. Had not known. He'd gone off on his
merry way, living a life that without her lacked flavor and
substance, but at least he'd been free to live his life as he
pleased.

Fiona . . . she was chained to that father of hers, chained
by bonds of promise and obligation that she had not been
willing to break.

Had she known she was pregnant when she left him that time here at Laramie? Had she swallowed both love and pride out of her sense of obligation to Brendan?

And had she come to despise Joe for the cruel twist his love had caused her? He could not blame her if she hated him now. He'd ruined her hopes, her dreams, indeed ruined her life. He would find no fault in her if she hated him now.

But he had to go to her. He had to see her. Explain that he had not known about the baby. His baby. *Their* child. He had to see her and he had to see the child they had created.

He did not know whether it was a boychild or a girl. Whether hale or weak. Whether it lived or died. Whether Fiona lived or died!

He had to find her. Had to see her. Had to find out about the baby. About the life he had so unknowingly pushed her into. He *had* to.

Joe felt an unfamiliar and distinctly uncomfortable heat behind his eyes as he yanked the cinches tight, gathered up his reins, and swung into the saddle.

The Sacramento, Crazy Henry said. That was where the Kramer train broke up.

That was where Joe would find Fiona. And his child.

He jabbed his heels into the Palouse horse's sides and lifted it into a canter even before he cleared the cluster of buildings at old Fort Laramie.

✤ 43 ✤

COMING DOWN INTO California from the Sierras, the Palouse lost its footing and went to its knees. The horse was used up. Joe had been perfectly willing to kill it in exchange for speed, and he damn near had.

The arid miles and dry, moisture-sucking winds of western Wyoming were hard enough on a horse. The flats of Utah were worse, and they only led to the high desert of Nevada. Lastly, the terrible heights and rocky trails of the towering mountains. Each had taken a toll on the Palouse's great stamina. Now it was nearing its end, its great heart overtaxed and flagging.

Joe stepped out of the saddle when the animal fell. He cursed and he fumed, but no amount of human anxiety would make things any different from what they were. The Palouse would carry him no further.

"Damn you!" he railed, but to no avail. "Damn you."

The horse tried to rise, its forefeet splayed wide seeking balance, but balance was no substitute for strength. It tried twice and then subsided, nostrils flared and sides pumping wildly, without rhythm.

"Damn you," Joe murmured, but gently this time. "You tried, boy. You gave me everything you had."

By rights he ought to put the creature out of its misery. He knew that. But the fault here was his.

So many faults were his, it seemed. So many. Ah, Fiona, what . . .

Joe shook that off. He had no time for recrimination now. He needed to find her. Needed to put right the wrongs he had done.

"Lay easy, boy. Let me help you."

Joe laid his Henry rifle aside and quickly loosed the cinch straps. He managed to pull the saddle and blanket, and stripped his headstall and bit from the Palouse's head.

"I don' know if you can make it, fella, but I'll give you your chance."

Joe pulled the packsaddle off the tough little mule that had trailed at the end of a lead rope everywhere the Palouse went. The mule was weary, but still strong after making the same journey but carrying far less weight.

He dumped his packs beside the trail, all his camp gear and the few eatables he still possessed, everything but saddle, weapons, and the cash in his pouch.

He saddled the mule and with a little trepidation—for he'd never bothered to ask if the animal were trained to ride—climbed onto it.

The mule swung its muzzle around to look at him. Joe braced himself for a storm, but the anticipated blowup never came. The mule just stood awaiting his signals. Joe bumped the little animal's sides with his heels and resumed his trek down into the green, lush spread of California that lay before him.

* * *

Wiggin's Station had grown since Joe last saw it. But then he was last here some years back, and thousands upon thousands of emigrants would have passed through here since that time. Somewhere among all those people would be Fiona McCarthy. And, he fervently hoped, the child he had given her.

"You look familiar," the proprietor of the mercantile said when Joe walked in. The man was named Amos. Joe could not recall his last name, but remembered that whatever it was, it was not Wiggin, and that he resented people making the assumption that it was.

"I been here before," Joe admitted.

Amos squinted. "Is there a train coming in? I didn't hear of one."

"No train. Leastways not with me. I passed a fourteen-wagon string early this week. They should be along by an' by."

Amos nodded. "Anybody I'd know leading them?"

"Some amateur. I didn't ask his name, the dumb son of a bitch. He lost more'n half his people along the way. Indians, sickness, hell, a couple of them even managed to get themselves drowned."

Amos sighed. "Every man's got the right to be as stupid as he pleases."

"True words, friend."

"What can I do for you." Amos tilted his head and squinted. "Moss, isn't it? Joe Moss?"

"Ayuh, that's me."

"What can I do for you, Moss?"

"I could use somethin' to eat. Some grub to carry along with me when I leave. An' some information. If I can only have one o' those things, then it'd be the information that I need more'n anything else."

"The food I can give you. Remains to be seen if I can help with the information, though."

"A man name of Brendan McCarthy and his daughter Fiona. They come through here about four years ago with a company guided by Henri Dubois. Man name of Kramer was president of the company."

Amos thought for a moment, then nodded. "I remember them. Kramer anyway. I can't say I recall anybody named McCarthy, though."

"D'you know where I can find Kramer?"

"Mm, yes, I think so. I heard he went up-valley and started him a store on the lower Feather. Settlement called Queensbury."

"Queensbury?"

Amos shrugged. "Don't ask me. I don't know where they come up with these names. Hangtown, for Christ's sake. Whoever would want to live in a town called something like that. This one somebody decided to call Queensbury."

Joe hadn't been questioning the wisdom of the name. He couldn't care less about anything like that. He'd just wanted to make sure he got the name right when he went looking for it. "North, you said."

"That's right. Pretty much due north from here, someplace on the Feather River."

"I'll find it," Joe said firmly. "Wherever it is, mister, I expect to find it. Now I'd like a hot meal and something to carry along that won't take much fixing. Dried meat maybe. Pemmican. Whatever you got."

"You'd eat pemmican? Man, that stuff tastes like shit."

"Yes, it does, but it'll keep damn near forever and it has enough fat in it to get a man through winter. You got any?"

"A little. I took some in on a trade. But that's been a couple years ago. You can have that cheap if you want it."

"I'll take it," Joe said. "Dried meat too if you got some.

Oh, and some cartridges for this here Henry rifle if you got any of those." He had shot some game on the way over from Fort Laramie, and he did not want to run short of the stubby brass self-contained cartridges.

"Mister, I heard there was such a gun as that, but I never saw one before right this minute. You might be able to find those cartridge things in San Francisco. I can't think of anyplace else this side of the States where they might have them, though."

"That isn't important anyway," Joe said. He meant it. Once he found Fiona and convinced her to marry him, his wandering days were done. He would settle for farming, maybe doing a little trading on the side. Maybe even start his own store like Samuel Kramer seemed to have done.

With Fiona beside him—and their baby too—Joe Moss figured he could do damn near anything.

"I'll take the grub then, an' if you don't mind I'm in kinda a hurry." He was smiling when he said that, smiling with eagerness and for the first time in ages, with a sense of growing optimism and exuberance. Close. He was so close now to Fiona and to their child.

Yes, he was very much in a hurry now.

✢ 44 ✢

JOE FELT A flutter of apprehension deep in his chest. Nervousness. It felt strange. But then it had been a very long time since anything had been as important as this.

Why, Brendan McCarthy and Fiona might live right here in this same small community. It could be the whole train of emigrants came here together to take up land. To farm and to build. And to raise their children.

Beyond Samuel Kramer's sprawling store was a large tree with a knotted rope hanging from one of the lower limbs. The ground beneath the rope was scuffed bare. By small feet. Children played here. Perhaps Joe and Fiona's baby among them? Or was it—he or she—too young? But it could be. It could be, Joe convinced himself. He felt a tightness in his chest.

He stepped down off the mule and tied it to a rail that was provided for the purpose. Self-consciously brushed himself off. And walked inside the store.

"You son of a bitch, what are you doing here?"

Joe stopped where he was, but he did not turn and leave. He would take any abuse, anything, if only he could find out where Brendan and Fiona were now.

"Murderer. Adulterer. What are you doing in my store, sinner? Get out. Get out, I say."

Joe's hand tightened on the grip of the Henry until his knuckles turned white, but he made no move to leave.

"Out, damn you!"

"I have to talk to you."

"I have nothing to say to the likes of you. You murdered my Tommy. You despoiled that child and left her. Now you walk in here and want to talk? Well, you'll not get any satisfaction from me, you son of a bitch."

A woman who had been quietly looking at a bolt of yard goods dropped the cloth she'd been holding, gave Samuel a stricken look, and scurried out of the store with her lips set in a tight, thin line. That was one customer who was unlikely to come back to Kramer's General Merc, Joe thought.

"I didn't know," Joe said softly. "I never knew. I only found out a few weeks ago. That's why I'm here. I want to make things right."

"And my Tommy? How do you propose to make that right, Moss?"

"I was not with Tommy that night, Samuel, or I would have defended him. Surely you know that. I told you then and I tell you now, I am sorry for your loss. But I did not do it. I did not cause it. Those young bucks did. They did it and they ran before anyone knew they were around. Before you knew and before I did. No one is to blame, Samuel, no one but the ones who did the murder, and no amount of sorrow or regret will change what was done that night."

"It seems to me there was a great deal of wrong done that night, Moss."

"I know that, Samuel, and you are right. I did not know.

You must understand that. You must believe me when I tell you that I did not know. I . . . I would have married the girl then. I want to marry her now. That is why I am here today. I want to find them. I want to make things right for them."

"I cannot help you, Moss. I don't know as I would if I were capable of it."

"Just tell me where they are, Samuel. I beg you. No matter what you think of me, think of Fiona. Think of the child. Tell me where they are. I want to make it right by them. For them, Samuel, not for me. Tell me where I can find them."

Some—a little—of the stiffness went out of Kramer's jaw and shoulders. The man had aged badly in the years since his son was killed, Joe realized. But then Kramer had nothing to live and hope for now. Joe hadn't really understood that. Now, with a child of his own to think about, he was beginning to understand that.

"Please, Samuel."

"I do not know for sure. When the train broke up and the company was dissolved, we scattered. There were more than sixty wagons if you remember. We did not all come here. Only four families did, my own included, and one of them has since moved on. McCarthy . . . let me try to remember. I think McCarthy and his daughter intended to go into the mining camps. Bryson might know something of them. He used to play cards with McCarthy. They were about as close as anyone ever got with Brendan."

"Where can I find Bryson then, Samuel?"

"He has a farm about three miles from here. Northwest. There is a road you can follow."

"Thank you, Samuel. Thank you very much."

"I still despise you, Moss. I want you to know that."

"Yes. I reckon I do know that, but I'm in your debt nonetheless." Joe turned toward the door, then stopped and turned back again. "One more thing, Samuel."

"Yes?" Some of the stiffness returned to the set of Kramer's shoulders.

"The child. Was it a boy or a girl?"

Kramer shook his head. "I would not know about that. The girl was still carrying it when I last saw them."

"Yes, well . . . thank you." Joe broke into a trot on his way to reclaim the mule and be on his way to Pat Bryson's farm.

"Yeah, I remember you." Bryson was a thin, ragged man wearing nothing but a pair of overalls and a sullen attitude. "Thought you was hot shit. Found out you wasn't, din' you."

Joe knew better than to argue with him. That would only set him off the worse. And now Joe remembered Bryson too, although he was the sort one would want to forget. "I'm looking for a friend of yours," Joe told him.

"You lookin' for Bren McCa'thy, ain't you?"

"Yeah. I am."

"Lookin' for that snooty bitch o' his. Well, you're lookin' in the wrong place for either one of 'em. They damn sure ain't around here no more."

Joe felt an impulse to take Bryson by the throat and squeeze. He kept his expression impassive and his hands down.

"Tol' Bren he shoulda married her off t' me 'stead o' that T-T-Thomas fella. But no. Ol' Bren thought he was gonna have him a piece o' a gold mine. Stupid bassard. You want a drink?"

Joe was taken somewhat aback by that suggestion. He was beginning to realize, though, that Bryson was already more than halfway toward being drunk. "D'you have a jug. Pat? I'd have a drink with you."

"I run out."

"Know where we can get some more?"

Bryson gave him a cagey look. Or anyway, what the man probably thought was a cagey look. "Could be."

"I'm buying," Joe said, and Bryson immediately began to smile.

"Always liked you, Moss, always did."

"Let's go buy us a bottle."

"Jus' a minute." Bryson disappeared inside his shack. He came back a moment later carrying a crockery jug that probably held half a gallon or more. "'S' empty," he explained.

"Uh-huh."

Bryson led the way on foot down a well-worn path that skirted around a hog pen and a tiny, poorly tended truck garden. The man's source of liquor was a neighbor who apparently offered a number of less savory services. Including Injun whiskey at four dollars a jug. Joe paid for the whiskey. Pat Bryson carried it, cradling the jug to his belly as if it were precious. Hell, to him it probably was. They walked down by the river to find some shade and drink it.

"T' yer health," Bryson said before he tipped the jug. He took a long swallow, shook himself with a scowl, and then began to smile. The world was commencing to look bright again, it seemed. "Have a drink."

Joe helped himself. The whiskey was no better than he might have expected, but no worse either. It landed in his belly like fire and continued to glow there. "That's good. You better have some more."

"Yeah, thanks."

"Mind if I ask you something, Pat?"

"Sure. You ast me anythin', Joe."

"Your buddy Bren. Where can I find him?"

"Dunno. Not no more."

"I thought he lived somewhere around here."

"Oh, he did. Him an' that butter-wouldn'-melt-in-her-mouth daughter o' his. Had them a claim. Good claim, mind you. Upriver a piece."

"A gold claim?"

"Tha's right. Gold." Bryson snorted. And took another drink. "Thought he was gonna be rich. You know? Gave T-T-Thomas Beadle that redheaded bitch t' take t' wife." Joe felt like he'd been kicked in the belly. Fiona was married?

Bryson drank some more. "Got half Beadle's claim." Bryson cackled as if something was funny. "Know what happened?" -

"No, I don't know, Pat." Joe reached for the jug, helped himself to a small snort, and passed the whiskey back to Bryson. "Why don't you tell me."

"Laugh was on Bren." He belched. "Laugh was on him a' right. Wa'n't hardly no gold left. Damn claim was played out. Sold that girl for nothing but hard work an' no money." Bryson blinked owlishly. "Not that she was worth s' much. She was knocked up, y'know. Did you know that, Joe? She was bellied up awful big. Beadle tooken her anyways. Prob'ly figured she wouldn't always be knocked up. Or anyway, if she was, then the nex' time it woulda been his nit she was carryin'."

Joe did not want to hear any more of this. "So what happened after that, Pat? You said Brendan and the girl don't live around here any more. How come they to leave?"

"Bren, he felt like he'd been cheated, tha's what happened. An' T-T-Thomas, he wanted his wife t' do for him, not fer her daddy. Bren didn' like that. Him and T-T-Thomas got into it pretty bad."

"Yes?"

"One night they had them a few drinks. Got them a jug. Next thing T-T-Thomas was laying on the floor with 'is gizzard cut outa him."

"Brendan killed him?"

"That's what they say. Him or the daughter, one of them done for him. They lit out from this country that night. Ain't been seen aroun' here since." The cagey look came over Pat Bryson again. He leaned close, his breath foul, and in a hoarse whisper said, "But I know where they went."

"Do you, Pat? Where would that be."

"Fella . . . fella I know . . . played cards with me an' Bren sometimes . . . fella I know seen Bren one time after. Year, maybe two after. Acrost the moun-teens in . . . whadda they call it . . . 'Ginia City. That's it. 'Ginia City. Excep' Bren wasn't calling himself McCa'thy no more. Took him some other name. I dunno what."

"And the girl? What about Fiona?"

Bryson shrugged. "Dunno, Joe. I dunno about her."

"Do you at least know if she had the baby? Was it . . . is it . . . a boy or a girl? Can you at least tell me that?"

Bryson blinked and helped himself to a long pull from the jug. "I dunno about that shit. She wasn't never no never-mind o' mine."

"And they lived in this 'Ginia City place?"

"Ver," Bryson said.

"What?"

"You ain't pernouncing it right. It's Ver-ginia City. Tha's where they live."

"Virginia City? Like in Nevada?" Joe had passed by close to there when he followed the Truckee into the Sierras on his way here.

"Tha's right. Just what I said. 'Ginia City. Hey! Joe. Where you going, buddy? Don't you want 'nuther drink?"

Joe did not even hear him. He was hurrying back to Bryson's place to reclaim the mule, already planning ahead. He would need a horse. And supplies enough to get him through to the Comstock country.

But, oh, Fiona! What had that miserable bastard of a father of hers done to her? And to their baby?

Where were they? How were they?

Joe did not even know what name they might be using now that Brendan was on the run for murdering his partner, Fiona's husband.

That thought squeezed Joe's gut and put an iron band around his heart. Poor Fiona. Dear Fiona. And it was his fault. All his fault.

If only he had known . . .

He shook that thought off and picked up his pace. He did not know then. Now he did. Now it was up to him to find Fiona and their child and to make things right for her. For the rest of her life he would make things right for her.

He swore it.

As soon as he found her. And he would never, not ever stop looking until his beloved Fiona was in his arms again and their baby with her.

Joe was running by the time he reached the place where he'd left the little mule.

PETER BRANDVOLD

*"Make room on your shelf of favorites:
Peter Brandvold will be staking out a claim there."*
—Frank Roderus

*"Recommended to anyone who loves the West as
I do. A very good read."* —Jack Ballas

*"Takes off like a shot, never giving the reader a chance to set
the book down."* —Douglas Hirt

AN EPIC WESTERN FROM THE AUTHOR OF
THE GUN

VENGEANCE GUN

BY **LYLE BRANDT**

JUSTICE HAS A NEW PRICE. MATT PRICE.

RETIRED GUNMAN MATT PRICE'S IDYLLIC WORLD HAS
SHATTERED WHEN A DANGEROUS GANG OF ROBBERS
TAKE THE ONE LIFE HE HOLDS DEAR—HIS WIFE'S.

NOW HE'S ON THE TRAIL AGAIN, HUNTING THE
MURDEROUS THIEVES WHO CRUELLY STOLE HIS PEACE.
HE'S THROUGH LIVING BY THE LETTER OF THE LAW—IT'S
TIME TO FOLLOW HIS OWN RULES, AND GIVE THIS GANG
THE TYPE OF PUNISHMENT THEY REALLY DESERVE.

0-425-19383-7

AVAILABLE WHEREVER BOOKS ARE SOLD OR AT
PENGUIN.COM

THE EPIC WESTERN FROM THE AUTHOR OF
THE GUN

JUSTICE GUN

LIVE BY IT. DIE BY IT.

BY **LYLE BRANDT**

GUNMAN MATTHEW PRICE DID NOT
THINK HE WAS GOING TO MAKE IT OUT OF
REDEMPTION, TEXAS, ALIVE.
BUT AS HE STUMBLES OUT OF TOWN
GUT-SHOT AND DYING, HE IS RESCUED BY A
BLACK FAMILY PIONEERING THEIR WAY TO
FREEDOM. NOW, MATT MUST RETURN THE
FAVOR AND HELP THEM WHEN
TROUBLEMAKERS IN THEIR NEW SETTLEMENT
OFFER UP A NOT-SO-WARM WELCOME.

0-425-19094-3

B678